Stories, sayings, and scriptures to Encourage and In

hugs™

to Brighten Your Day

闪亮的日子

Ashley Moore &
Korie Robertson
LeAnn Weiss 著

李克议 主译
郑红 杨斌

HOWARD
PUBLISHING CO.

[皖] 版贸登记号:1208543

图书在版编目(CIP)数据

拥抱·爱. 闪亮的日子:英汉对照/(美)穆尔(Moore, A.),(美)罗伯逊(Robertson, K.)著;李克议主译. —合肥:安徽科学技术出版社,2009.1

ISBN 978-7-5337-4271-3

Ⅰ.拥… Ⅱ.①穆…②罗…③李… Ⅲ.①英语-汉语-对照读物②故事-作品集-美国-现代 Ⅳ.H319.4:Ⅰ

中国版本图书馆 CIP 数据核字(2008)第 198270 号

拥抱·爱.闪亮的日子:英汉对照

(美)穆尔(Moore, A.),(美)罗伯逊(Robertson, K.)著　　李克议 主译

出 版 人:黄和平
责任编辑:田　斌
封面设计:朱　婧
出版发行:安徽科学技术出版社(合肥市政务文化新区圣泉路 1118 号
　　　　　出版传媒广场,邮编:230071)
电　　话:(0551)3533330
网　　址:www.ahstp.net
E - mail:yougoubu@sina.com
经　　销:新华书店
排　　版:安徽事达科技贸易有限公司
印　　刷:合肥华星印务有限责任公司
开　　本:787×1240　1/32
印　　张:6
字　　数:77 千
版　　次:2009 年 1 月第 1 版　2009 年 1 月第 1 次印刷
印　　数:6 000
定　　价:16.00 元

给爱一个归宿
——出版者的话

身体语言是人与人之间最重要的沟通方式，而身体失语已让我们失去了很多明媚的"春天"，为什么不可以给爱一个形式？现在就转身，给你爱的人一个发自内心的拥抱，你会发现，生活如此美好！

肢体的拥抱是爱的诠释，心灵的拥抱则是情感的沟通，彰显人类的乐观坚强、果敢执著与大爱无疆。也许，您对家人、朋友满怀缱绻深情却羞于表达，那就送他一本《拥抱·爱》吧。一本书，七个关于真爱的故事；一本书，一份荡涤尘埃的"心灵七日斋"。一个个叩人心扉的真实故事，一句句震撼心灵的随笔感悟，从普通人尘封许久的灵魂深处走出来，在洒满大爱阳光的温情宇宙中尽情抒写人性的光辉！

"拥抱·爱"(Hugs)系列双语典藏读物是"心灵鸡汤"的姊妹篇，安徽科学技术出版社与美国出版巨头西蒙舒斯特携手倾力打造，旨在把这套深得美国读者青睐的畅销书作为一道饕餮大餐，奉献给中国的读者朋友们。

每本书附赠CD光盘一张，纯正美语配乐朗诵，让您在天籁之音中欣赏精妙美文，学习地道发音。

世界上最遥远的距离，不是树枝无法相依，而是相互凝望的星星却没有交会的轨迹。

"拥抱·爱"系列双语典藏读物，助您倾吐真情、启迪心智、激扬人生！

一本好书一生财富，今天你拥抱了吗？

For Macy, Ally,
Maddox, John Luke,
Sadie, Will, and Bella—
our children,
who always brighten
our day.

献给那些永远使我们的日子闪
亮的孩子们：他们是玛丝，艾丽，玛
德斯，威尔和贝勒

Contents

1

You are here
to enrich the world.

你来到这个世界，为之增彩，使之富有

Woodrow Wilson

·chapter one·

Reaching Out

1

伸出援手

Every day I am your
way, your truth, and
your life. You can reach
out because I strengthen
you in all you do. And as
you give, watch Me multiply
blessings back to you
in overflowing ways.

Generously,
Your God of Every Good
and Perfect Gift

—from John 14:6; Philippians 4:13; Luke 6:38; James 1:17

我每天都和你在一起，为你找真理，为你指明生活方向。你可以伸出双手拥抱，因为我总是为你做想做的一切。而当你做到这时，看着我为你做出的无限的祈祷，这将使你受益无尽。

你的慷慨的上帝，为你准备一切美好的礼物

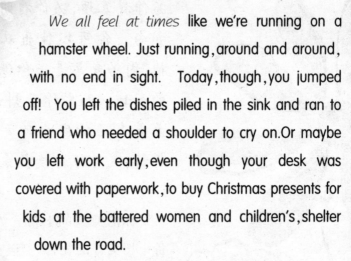

We all feel at times like we're running on a hamster wheel. Just running, around and around, with no end in sight. Today, though, you jumped off! You left the dishes piled in the sink and ran to a friend who needed a shoulder to cry on. Or maybe you left work early, even though your desk was covered with paperwork, to buy Christmas presents for kids at the battered women and children's, shelter down the road.

Whatever it was you did for someone else, it felt good. You traded all the tasks on your to-do list for something of greater significance. And you noticed something.

Nothing dreadful happened. The earth kept spinning on

its axis. No natural disasters could be traced
back to your change in schedule.

In fact, sometimes it's exactly when life seems
to be spinning out of control—when you just don't
think you could possibly help anybody else because
your life is such a mess—it's exactly then that we
need to reach out. Somehow you just do it, and
afterward you know why it pays to go the extra
mile.

Who knows but that you really needed
that walk more than the person who
asked you to join her. At any rate, it
sure beats running on the wheel

有时我们会感到自己就像转轮里的小仓

鼠,不停地在跑,一圈又一圈,却没有尽头。但是今天,

你终于跳出来了,可以把成堆的碗碟留在洗碗池,去找一

个需要帮助的朋友,或是把工作放在一边,提前回家,去

路边的"妇幼之家"给孩子们采购圣诞礼物。

　　不管你为别人做了什么事情,都会让你的心

情变好。你可以把备忘清单上的工作全部

换成其他更有意义的事情。你会注

意到, 其实并没有什么糟

糕的事情发生,

　　　　地 球

也仍在正常旋转,同样,也没有任何自然灾

害因为你的改变而引起。

　　很多时候,你觉得自己的生活已是一团糟,没办法再

去帮助别人。其实,正是由于生活已偏离了轨道,我们才

更应该伸出援助之手。只有你做过之后,才会明白,多

做这一点是值得的。

　　说不定你从其中的获益,要远多于向

你求助之人。不管怎样,这至少比

在转轮里无尽的跑圈要

好得多。

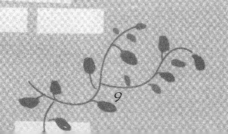

*I have learned
that what we have done
for ourselves alone dies with us.
What we have done for others and
the world remains and is immortal.*

Albert Pike

我现在明白我们只为我们自己所
做的一切将和我们一起灭亡，而我们
为别人以及为这个世界所做的一切将
和我们同在，并且永存。

This is only for a little while, Cheryl kept telling herself. But she was at the end of her rope.

这只是一小会儿，谢丽尔不断地对自己说。但是她已忍无可忍了。

The Gift

The phone rang as Cheryl was starting another load of laundry. It was the third one she'd done that day, along with cleaning the bathrooms, vacuuming the entire house, mopping the kitchen floor, and taking care of the three children—all while her husband sat in his home office leisurely working at the computer. Cheryl had thought Gary's going into business for himself and having his office at home would be great for the family. But now she realized all that meant was that her husband never left work. Working was all he seemed to be doing these days.

"I'm not answering! " Cheryl hollered to Gary. "I don't have time to talk to anyone." She knew she sounded haggard. That was how she felt, and she wanted Gary to know it. Today was Saturday. She'd been trying to make her feelings known all week.

"Ring, ring, this is the Stone residence. Sorry we missed your call..." Cheryl could hear the answering machine from the hall. *Figures,* she thought. *Gary can't even take the time to answer the phone around here.* Then she muttered under her breath to whoever might be calling. "Don't hold your breath. 'As soon as possible' is gonna be a while."

Gary had decided to quit his job to become an independent contractor three months earlier with Cheryl's full support. He had plenty of computer expertise, and they felt confident he could get enough consulting-work to make a good living. She just hadn't realized how hard he would have to work to make that happen.

For all her grumpiness, Cheryl knew Gary was a good husband. He'd always participated fully with the three children, waking up for nighttime feedings when they were babies, taking turns shuttling the oldest to school and practice for whatever sport was in season. He'd stop by the grocery store or the pizza place on the way home from work to pick up supper, and he'd throw in a load or two of laundry when necessary. They had been a good-team—always busy, but somehow it had worked. Until recently.

Cheryl understood that Gary was feeling the burden of responsibility to make it in his new venture and be able to support the family. *This is only for a little while, until he gets going,* she kept telling herself. But lately the positive self-talk was being drowned out by self-pity. *Sure, he's working, but I work fullt-time too, plus I'm doing everything else around here.* Their second-grader

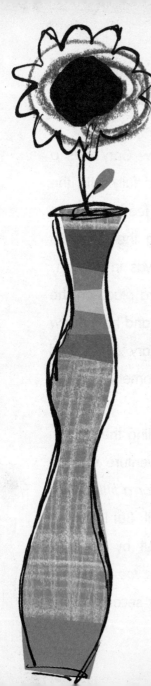

had homework at least a couple of nights a week, and the twin toddlers were a handful— the house seemed in a continual state of disaster. Cheryl was worn out and at the end of her rope. And when Gary, didn't answer the phone, it felt like the last straw.

Her mental grumbling was interrupted by the voice on the answering machine. "Cheryl, this is Laura. I was hoping we could do something fun together this evening. I really need a break from the hospital and could use someone to talk to."

Cheryl immediately felt awful. That was her best friend in the entire world. Laura's father had had a stroke on Monday. The doctors didn't think he would ever fully recover. Cheryl had gone to the hospital when it happened but had been so busy since then that she'd hardly even checked on Laura, except for one measly call to ask how her dad was doing.

I have to call her back, she thought, *but there's no way I can go.* There was more laundry to do, bills to pay, and groceries to shop for. Besides, who would watch the kids? If she left them home while Gary was working, they'd just destroy the house she'd worked all day to clean. She'd never get all the chores done before the new week started and they piled up all over again. She picked up the phone to somehow gracefully decline the invitation.

"When are you leaving?" Gary hollered.

"What do you mean, when am I leaving?" she retorted, not bothering to disguise her aggravation.

"I mean, I think you should go," Gary said with a smile as he joined her in the kitchen. "I'll stay home with the kids and keep the laundry going and do whatever else was on your list for the day."

"But what about your work?"

17

"It can wait. Your friend is more important. Besides, you need a little fun in your life too."

I couldn't agree more! she thought. "I don't know what's gotten into you, but I'll take you up on that offer!" Cheryl hugged her husband and happily picked up the phone to dial her best friend before he had a chance to change his mind.

After a quick conversation and a plan for Cheryl to pick up Laura at the hospital so they could ride together and talk on the way to the restaurant, Cheryl threw on some lipstick, slipped on her boots, kissed the kids goodbye, and was out the door. She turned around quickly though, poked her head back inside, and yelled, "Don't forget to give the kids baths so they're clean for church in the morning." Her step was feeling a little lighter, but the knot in her stomach that had grown and tightened over the past few months was still there.

When she arrived at the hospital, Cheryl was struck by what a difficult thing Laura must be going through. She was an only child, and she had lost her mother just two years before. Somehow, though, Cheryl couldn't quite stop her mind from drifting back to her own problems.

"Thanks so much for rescuing me," Laura said as she met her friend at the front desk. "I can't tell you how much I needed this."

"Well, I have to admit, my life has been crazy lately, and getting away seemed almost too monumental a task when I first heard your message." Then, guiltily, "But I always have time for you."

As the two friends walked through the parking garage, the conversation kept going back to Cheryl and how stressful her situation was. She knew she should be letting her friend vent instead of complaining. But she couldn't stop worrying about whether her husband was really doing what he said he would or if he had slipped back to his office. She was going to lose it if she came home to a houseful of chores and dirty children.

As they approached the car, she noticed Laura looking in the window of an old, brown Chevy Caprice

that had definitely seen better days. Cheryl muttered an attempt at humor, "I think they need to haul that clunker off to the junkyard."

But Laura didn't laugh. She started rummaging in her overcrowded purse. Cheryl saw her friend pull out a paper from her wallet and lean into the open window of the "clunker."

"Oh! " Cheryl stuttered. "I—I hope I didn't offend you by making fun of that car. Were you leaving a note for someone you know?"

"No," Laura replied somewhat mysteriously. "Come on; let's go enjoy a wonderful meal. I'm sick of hospital food."

But Cheryl's curiosity was aroused. She came around to where Laura was standing and peeked into the window of the old car. A bright yellow notice with a red FINAL stamp on it was lying face-up on the seat. It was an electric bill for $98.99. Then something else caught her eyes. Tucked under that notice, just barely showing, was the corner of what looked like money.

The Gift

Cheryl knew instantly what Laura had done. Her friend had always been kind-hearted, but seeing her do something that generous in the midst of such a difficult time in her life brought tears to Cheryl's eyes. *What a contrast to my wallowing in self-pity,* she thought, ashamed. Today, while she'd been busy thinking only of herself, her husband had set aside what he was doing and thought of her. And her friend, who was in the midst of her own turmoil, had listened to Cheryl's little grievances and helped someone she didn't even know. It was a living illustration of how to set aside her problems and think of someone else.

She turned and hugged Laura as tightly as she could. "Thanks, Laura."

"For what? I didn't give *you* the money," Laura joked. "For reminding me how truly blessed I am."

礼　物

　　电话响起的时候，谢丽尔正要开始洗下一堆衣服。这已经是今天的第三堆衣服了。之前她还一个人清理了整个浴室，打扫完所有房间，擦干净了厨房的地板，还安顿好了三个孩子，而在这期间，她的丈夫盖瑞却是一直悠闲地坐在他的电脑前工作。谢丽尔曾经认为让盖瑞在家创业对这个家来说是件好事，但是现在她才意识到，这样做的后果便是，她丈夫再无休假一说。工作已经成了他这些日子里唯一在做的事情。

　　"我接不了电话！"谢丽尔大声喊道，"我现在顾不上。"她知道这么说话让人听起来很烦。但这正是她现在的感受，她就是想让盖瑞知道。今天是星期六，一周以来她一直想让盖瑞知道她心里在想什么。

　　"铃……铃……这里是斯通家，很抱歉我们没有接到您的电话……",谢丽尔听到了大厅里答录机的回复声。"我就知道。"谢丽尔想,"盖瑞居然连抬手接电话的时间都没有。"然后她又对那个还在打电话的人嘟囔着说:"别等了,'尽快'的意思就是还有一会儿。"

三个月前,盖瑞决定辞去工作,做一个独立承包商,对此谢丽尔也曾表示完全支持。盖瑞对电脑尤为擅长,所以他们都认为他可以接到许多咨询业务,日子也会好起来。然而当时她却没有想到,要实现这些,他需要非常辛苦地工作。

尽管谢丽尔抱怨连连,但她也知道盖瑞是个好丈夫。例如在照顾三个孩子方面,他就分担了许多。孩子刚出生时,他会在夜里起床喂奶。大儿子上学也是他们轮番接送,他还会带孩子去练习时下流行的各种运动。在下班途中,他会去食品店或比萨店买晚饭回家。在她忙的时候,他还会帮忙洗些衣服。他们曾经是一对好搭档,虽然忙,但生活还算美满,直到现在才变得不同。

谢丽尔明白盖瑞想在这份新工作上一展身手,让家里过得更好些,肩负的担子非常重。"这不会太久的,等他工作步入正轨就好了。"她一直这样对自己说。但是最近这种自我鼓励已经沦为了自我安慰。"当然,他是在工作。但是我也是做全职工作啊,而且我还要做家里所有的事情!"他们上二年级的大儿子每周至少两个晚上有家庭作业,那两个刚会走路的小家伙更是一对小麻烦——整个家里似乎总是处于灾难的状态。谢丽尔对此已经筋疲力尽、束手无策了。这次盖瑞不去接电话,她终于要爆发了。

这时，答录机里面的说话声打断了她的愤恨思绪："谢丽尔，我是劳拉。今晚你陪我去找点乐子吧。我太需要从医院这些琐事中解脱出来，找个人说说话了。"

谢丽尔的情绪马上变得沮丧起来，这是她在这个世界上最好的朋友。劳拉的爸爸周一的时候突然中风，医生认为很难痊愈。当天谢丽尔就赶往医院看望了，但是从那以后她就再没有抽得出时间联系劳拉，甚至连个问候的电话也没有。

"我必须给她打个电话。"她想，"但是我没办法去啊。"家里还有一大摞衣服要洗，一厚叠账单要付，一大堆东西要买。此外，又有谁来照顾孩子们呢？她离开了，而盖瑞在工作，这群小家伙会把她辛苦了一天的劳动成果给毁掉的。这样她就完成不了家务，而新的一周又要开始，它们会越积越多的……她拿起电话，打算委婉地把约会推掉。

"你什么时候走啊？"盖瑞大声问道。

"你说什么？我什么时候走？"她回过神来，并没有刻意掩饰她刚才的愤怒。

"我的意思是，我觉得你应该去。"盖瑞走进厨房，微笑地对她说，"我会待在家里照看孩子，继续洗衣服，并把你今天家务清单上剩下的活干完。"

"但是你自己的工作呢？"

"不急。你的朋友更重要呢。再说，你也应该去找点乐子了。"

"非常正确！"她想。"不知道你怎么想的，但我决定接受你的

建议！"谢丽尔开心地抱着他说，然后迅速抓起电话拨了过去，以免他又改变了主意。

简短的通话后，她们决定由谢丽尔先开车到医院接劳拉，然后去吃饭，她们可以在路上边走边聊。谢丽尔涂上唇膏，穿了靴子，跟小家伙们吻别后就出门了。不过她又马上转回身，把头伸进门嚷道："别忘了给孩子们洗澡，明天早晨我们要去教堂做礼拜。"她的脚步轻松了许多，但是过去几个月里一直纠缠在心里的结仍然没有彻底解开。

谢丽尔在赶到医院之后，才明白劳拉面临的处境多么艰难。她是家里唯一的孩子，她妈妈两年前又刚刚去世。然而即便如此，谢丽尔的脑子里，还是抑制不住地重复着每天烦扰自己的那堆麻烦。

"太感谢你来拯救我了。"劳拉在前台接到她时说，"你不知道我是多么需要你来。"

"唉，说实话，最近我的生活太糟糕了，在听到你的留言之前，我还忙得抽不开身呢。"然后她马上又违心地说，"但是说到陪你，我总是有时间的。"

在她们走到停车场后，话题又回到了谢丽尔忙乱的生活上。她知道她现在应该是让自己的朋友发泄，而不是自己在抱怨。然而她禁不住地担心，她丈夫是按他所说的在做家务呢，还是又溜回到了办公桌前。如果回到家里发现还有一大堆家务没做，孩子也没洗澡，她会发狂的。

这时，她注意到劳拉停在了一辆老式的棕色"雪佛兰·荣"旁

边,显然它已经历了许多岁月。谢丽尔开玩笑地说:"我想他们应该把这辆老爷车拖到废品场去。"

但是劳拉没有笑,开始在鼓鼓囊囊的手提包里翻找起来。谢丽尔注意到她的朋友从钱包里掏出一张什么纸,从这辆"老爷车"开着的窗户放了进去。

"啊!"谢丽尔结巴地说,"我……我想我不该取笑这辆车的,你没生气吧。你要不要给你这个朋友留个纸条?"

"不用。"劳拉有些神秘地说,"走吧,我们去吃顿好的,我已经受不了医院的伙食了。"

但是谢丽尔的好奇心已经被吊起来了。她绕到刚才劳拉站的地方,透过车窗往里看,发现座位上有一张正面朝上的黄色通知单,上面贴着一个鲜红的"最后通知"标签,是张98.99元的电费单。这时她注意到通知单下面有个几乎被完全盖住的东西,从折起的边角来看,似乎是张钱。

谢丽尔突然明白了刚才劳拉做了什么。她的朋友一向很热心。但是此时此刻,劳拉自己处境也很困难,却还是去慷慨地帮助别人,此种举动让谢丽尔泪流不已。"而我却总是一味地自怜,这是多大的不同啊!"她感到非常羞愧。今天她一直只是顾着考虑她自己,但她的丈夫却已放下手头的工作,来为她考虑。她的朋友也是,自己身处不幸之中,却也能倾听谢丽尔的牢骚,还会帮助那些素昧平生的人。这就是身边一个能应对自身问题又为他人考虑的现实的榜样。

她转过身,紧紧地抱住劳拉。"劳拉,谢谢你。"

"怎么了? 我没有把钱给'你'呀。"劳拉开玩笑说。

"因为你提醒了我自己是多么的幸福。"

Looking Up

·chapter two·

Looking Up

② 展望

Get the right perspective by looking up and remembering that I'm your power source. I'm watching over you and won't let you slip or fall. Nothing is too difficult for Me. Wait upon Me, and I'll renew you and help you to soar above the obstacles of life so you won't quit.

Encouraging you,
Your Heavenly Father

—from Psalm 121:2-5; Luke 1:37; Isaiah 40:31

向前看，你可以得到正确的前景，记住，我是你的力量源泉。我会关注你，不会让你摔倒，世上什么也难不倒我，等待我的到来，我将使你焕然一新，帮你度过生活中所有的障碍，你一定不要放弃。

鼓励你的,伟大的上帝

You give it all you're got. But in this world, all you've got isn't always good enough. Except with those who love you. For them your best is better than good enough. It's perfect!

There's something you don't hear very often. You, perfect? Well, in a way you are. Not that you always succeed or never make mistakes. But you're perfect in the sense that you're just the way God made you. Perfect, not because of anything you've done, but because you are the person He created you to be.

And what does He ask for in return? That you keep trying. That you do your best and look to Him when you need help.

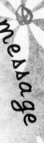

Sometimes relying on someone else is easier said than done. You've worked hard, and it's difficult to admit you need help. You're strong, self-sufficient. You want to stand on your own two feet. And that's good. All parents want their children to grow into strong, independent adults. Your heavenly Father is no different.

Just remember that like a loving parent, He also wants to be there for you. He's cheering for you. And He's waiting for your glance—ready for the time you look up to heaven, telling Him you need Him. Until then, He'll wait. He won't take His eyes off of you.

"你为之尽了全力。"但在这个世界上,

你所尽的全力并不总是足够好的。除了那些你爱的

人,只有对他们,你才会做出比"足够好"更大的努力,你

才会做到完美。

有个词你可能不常听到。你,完美?是的,在某种意义

上。并不是说你常胜不败或从不犯错,而是说你已经按

照上帝的意旨做到了最好。完美,并非由于你曾做

过什么,而是由于你顺从了上帝的意旨。

那么上帝又提出了什么条件作为

回报呢?你必须坚持不懈。你必

须尽你所能并在需要时

向他求助。

依赖

别人这种事有时候做起来要比说起来难。因为你已经付出了许多努力，所以很难接受自己需要帮助这个事实。你很坚强，能够自给自足，你只想依靠自己的力量，这些很好。所有的父母都希望自己的孩子成为坚强、独立的人。你的上帝父亲也一样。

　　要记得，上帝就像一个慈爱的父亲，他也想随时为你伸出帮助之手。他在为你加油，他在等待你的目光——等着你抬头望天，告诉他你需要他。他会等待，直到那一刻的到来。他的视线一刻也不会从你的身上离开。

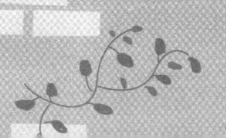

We bring nothing to God,

and He gives us everything.

我们没给上帝带去任何东西;而上帝却给了
我们一切

Gary Thomas

*R*obert stood there, longing for his daughter to give him just one glance.

罗伯特站在那，期望他的女儿看他最后一眼。

Out of the Sand

Robert's stomach was in knots. Watching his daughter bound down the runway to leap with all her might into the soft sand, he couldn't help but wonder how she was handling the pressure. She had told him coming home from regionals that when she jumped, the sand didn't feel soft at all; it felt like freshly poured concrete that had almost completely set up.

She had worked hard, training endlessly for today's event—the state track meet. This was Erin's senior year, her last chance, and her dream was there for the taking. Robert wanted his daughter to succeed, to achieve what she's worked so hard for. He'd coached and encouraged her along the way, but now there was nothing more he could do. He and his wife, Karen, could only stand there, knuckles white, grasping the yellow guard rail as Erin ran for her first jump.

She did! It looked good enough to Robert. Karen jumped up and down with pride and excitement. Although it was hard to tell from their place in the sands, he could see the beaming face of their only child and knew it must have been a good jump.

But her body language was saying something different. Instead of her usual dance like bound as she rose from the sand, Erin was moving slowly. This was not a good sign.

"I think she's hurt,"Karen said. Robert saw it too; he

responded with a silent mix of hope and concern. Erin had two more jumps to go, and while no one but her parents would have noticed, they could tell something wasn't right.

Erin was in second place at the end of round one, and Robert thought about the many times she had won after a more meager start. But watching his daughter's broken steps as she prepared for her second attempt, Robert's fears were confirmed. Erin was hurting.

"Erin Thompson up!" rang out from the loud speaker. As she ran down the runway, Robert rocked from side to side, feeling with his daughter each painful step.

She made the jump, but this time there was no smile—and certainly no bounce after her accomplishment. "Fourteen feet seven inches," the judge announced. Not as long as the first. Erin jammed her right hand into the sand and pushed herself up. Robert recognized the grim determination he'd often seen in his daughter.

"She's a fighter," Karen said under her breath, putting into words what Robert was thinking.

He laughed. "Remember when she was two ? Her favorite phrase was 'I do it myself! '" Robert was proud of Erin's strength but always wished she would lean on him and her mother at least a little. He stood there longing for his daughter to give him just one small glance, to look his way so he could tell her with his eyes just how proud he was of her, no matter what she did or what place she finished.

While most of the crowd talked and laughed, Robert stood statuesque, never taking his eyes off his daughter. If she should happen to look his way, he'd give her a big smile and a thumbs up to let her know he was there if she needed him.

"Round three! Erin Thompson up! " The call came all too quickly. Erin started down the runway, focused on the goal. Robert was focused on her. He nearly threw himself over the rail as she made the final jump. "Fourteen feet and five inches! " the judge yelled.

That may have been good enough for regionals, but it won't cut it for state, Robert thought. His heart sank, knowing how disappointed Erin would be.

"Top six to the finals, listen carefully for the names," the judge said. "Julia Jackson, Carmen Smith, Amy Rodgers, Samantha Kennedy, Casey Gaston, and in sixth place, Erin Thompson. You have thirty minutes to prepare."

Erin had never been in sixth place in anything her whole life. Robert saw the anger and disbelief on his daughter's face. Yet still no glance for which Robert longed as he watched his little girl limp the entire length of the track to the field house.

"I hate this," he told his wife.

"She'll be fine," she tried to assure him.

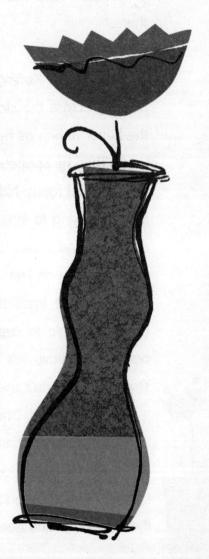

"I can't take it anymore," he said. "I'm going out there."

"Robert—"

The rest of Karen's words were lost. He was already halfway across the stands. His imagination was getting the better of him as he envisioned finding his daughter in tears. Then he spotted her. In the far right-hand corner of the crowded room, hidden behind the leg press machine, Erin was trying to stretch out. Robert could see that she couldn't bend down far on her left leg, but he saw no sign of defeat on Erin's face. She was set like stone.

He stood back for a moment, marveling at her valiant struggle to overcome the pain. He smiled and decided to leave her to her preparation. Just as he started to go, Erin's eyes met his.

"I can do this, Dad."

He nodded. "I know."

Robert walked back to the stands, his steps a little lighter. At least he had made contact. Erin knew he was there for her if she needed him.

He slid back into his seat beside Karen just in time to hear the voice from the loud speaker. "Girls' long jump!" His stomach tightened again as six athletically lean girls walked to the runway.   One had a look of elation, another seemed pensive,   but Erin had that familiar stare of pride and determination as she limped all the way.

Erin started warming up,   and Robert rose from his seat to assume his guardian stance. Karen stood beside him. "Has it been thirty minutes already?"

"I don't think she's ready," Robert muttered.

"She was born ready," was Karen's confident reply. Robert smiled, knowing she was right.

"Erin Thompson up! "

Even before the judge's announcement, Robert knew Erin's jump hadn't been long enough.

"Thirteen feet ten inches! "

His heart broke for his daughter, but he couldn't see any break in her spirit. She pounded both hands into the grainy sand and sprang up,   using only her right foot to carry the weight of her slender body.

Looking Up

"Come on, Erin, you can do it! " Robert yelled, hoping she would hear him and look up for a little support. But if Erint was listening, she didn't let on. She simply resumed her stretches, readying herself for the next jump.

Her distance was only getting lower, and this time Erin had to practically crawl out of the sand. It was almost too much to bear. She only had one more chance.

As all the other contestants went bounding down the runway one after another, Robert wished he could take this pressure away from his daughter, make it all better. Hug her and tell her it was fine, he loved her no matter what. If she didn't want to jump again, it was

OK. This was just a silly competition—it didn't really matter.

But he knew it did. Erin had worked hard for this, and nothing was going to keep her from giving her best—even if today her best wouldn't win a medal.

Erin slumped on the black asphalt, waiting her turn. "Just look at me, honey," Robert pleaded under his breath, hoping to pass her some kind of support from across the field.

The loud speaker blared. "This is your final jump. Erin Thompson up! "

Erin struggled to her place, and just before getting set, she looked up into the stands. Robert read her meaning. She knew they were there for her, and she was going to give it her all. He blinked to hide the mistiness of his eyes and stood grinning, cheering her on. "That's my girl! " he yelled. "Give 'em all you've got."

Her best had always been enough for him. But would it be enough for his competitive daughter? One last time, Erin took off down the runway, awkwardly striving for her goal.

Looking Up

"Thirteen feet even."

It was short.   But this time there was no hand—pounding.   There was no movement to get up from the sand.   Just a slow turn of the head to search out her father, looking for help. She needed him.

Robert hurdled the cold, yellow guard rail and sprinted to Erin's side. Tears of pain streaked her cheeks. Robert knelt and gently lifted her out of the sand. "I'm proud of you," he whispered in her ear. "Are you all right?"

"Of course I am. I did my best, and a girl can't do any better than that," Erin said proudly, though Robert could hear the pain in her voice.

"I knew that, but I wasn't sure if you knew it."

"Hey, what have you been teaching me all these years?" Erin said with a half–smile, half-grimace.

"That's my girl," Robert said unevenly, his voice betraying the depth of emotion and pride he felt. "That's my girl."

沙场之外

罗伯特紧张无比。看着女儿沿着跑道跳出去,奋力跳到沙坑里时,他忍不住想问她是怎么承受这种压力的。有一次从地区赛回到家里,她曾告诉过他说,跳远的时候沙坑感觉上去一点都不柔软,反而像是新倒的混凝土一样。

她训练得非常刻苦,无数次的训练就是为了今天的这次比赛——国家径赛运动会。爱瑞恩今年将毕业,这是她最后一次机会,她的梦想就是参加这次比赛。罗伯特衷心希望他的女儿能够成功,希望她长久的努力能得到回报。一直以来都是他在训练她,鼓励她,但现在已经没有什么他能做的了。他和妻子,凯伦,只能站在那儿,指节发白,紧紧抓住黄色的护栏,看着爱瑞恩第一跳开始助跑。

她做到了!在罗伯特看来这一跳很漂亮。妻子凯伦激动而自豪地跳了起来。虽然从他们在看台中的位置很难看到结果,但他能看到他们的独生女儿脸上那愉悦的表情,因此他知道这肯定是漂亮的一跳。

但她的动作看起来不太舒展。以往从沙坑中站起来时,她都会像跳舞一样轻轻一跳,但这一次她的动作却异常缓慢。这不是一个好迹象。

"我想她受伤了。"凯伦说。罗伯特也看到了;他只是静静地没有说话,带着些许期待,些许担忧。爱瑞恩还有两跳,虽然除了她的父母之外没人注意到,但他们两人能够看出,事情有点不对了。

第一轮结束后爱瑞恩排名第二,罗伯特想起以前也有很多次她的开局更加不利,但最终还是反败为胜了。但是当看到女儿在准备第二跳时那毫不流畅的步伐时,罗伯特的担心被证实了,爱瑞恩很疼。

"爱瑞恩·汤普森上场!"扩音器里发出了响亮的声音。当她在跑道上助跑的时候,罗伯特也左右摇晃着身体,与女儿一起体会她的每一步疼痛。

她跳了出去,但这一次没有了笑容——自然在跳完之后也没有那轻盈的舞蹈般的一跳。"14英尺7英寸。"裁判宣布。没有第一次跳得远。爱瑞恩右手伸到沙坑里,把自己撑了起来。罗伯特认出了以前经常在女儿脸上看到的那种坚定的决心。

"她真的很坚强。"凯伦声音低低的,说出了罗伯特心里的话。

他笑了起来。"还记得她两岁的时候吗?她最喜欢说的话就是

'我自己来'"。罗伯特对爱瑞恩的坚强非常自豪,却也一直希望她能稍微依赖一下他或她的母亲,哪怕只有一点点。他站在那里,期待女儿能往他这边看看,期待他的女儿能看他哪怕一眼,这样他就能用眼睛告诉她,他是多么为她骄傲,不管她做了什么,也不管她最终能取得什么成绩。

当大部分人在有说有笑的时候,罗伯特像个雕塑般站着,眼睛一刻也没有从女儿身上移开过。如果她碰巧往这边看过来,他将给她一个大大的微笑,然后伸出大拇指,让她知道如果她需要他将随时出现。

"第三轮!爱瑞恩上场!"扩音器的声音快得令人措手不及。爱瑞恩沿着跑道开始助跑,双眼紧紧盯着前面的目标。罗伯特则紧紧地盯着她。当她跳出最后一跳时,他也几乎将自己摔出了护栏。"14英尺5英寸。"裁判喊道。

这个成绩在地区赛中算是很好,但在国家赛中还不够,罗伯特想。他的心便沉了,知道爱瑞恩会有多么失望。

"前六名进入决赛,请仔细听选手名单,"裁判宣布说,"朱利安·杰克逊,卡门·史密斯,艾米·罗杰斯,瑟曼莎·肯尼迪,凯西·杰斯顿,还有第六名,爱瑞恩·汤普森。你们有30分钟准备时间。"

爱瑞恩从来没有在她生命中的任何事情中屈居过第六名。罗伯特看到了女儿脸上的怒气和难以置信。但是在看着女儿一路从赛道一瘸一拐的走进休息室的过程中,罗伯特始终没有收到他期盼的、女儿瞥来的一眼。

"我讨厌这样。"他对妻子说。

"她会没事的。"她试图向他保证。

"我受不了了，"他说，"我过去看看。"

"罗伯特——"

凯伦接下来的话他没有听到。他已经穿过了半个看台。当想象着看到女儿流泪的样子时，他的想象力战胜了他。然后他就找到了她。在拥挤的休息室右手边远远的一个角落里，爱瑞恩正在腿部按压机后面尽力舒展她的身体。罗伯特能看出她的身体用左腿没法弯下去很多，但是他在她的脸上并没有看到受挫的表情。她看上去就像一块顽石。

他在原地站了一会儿，对她克服疼痛的勇敢抗争感到惊奇。他笑了，决定留她自己去准备。正当他要离开的时候，爱瑞恩的视线与他的相遇了。

"我能行，爸爸。"

他点了点头，"我知道。"

罗伯特走回了看台，他的步伐轻松了一些。至少他已经跟她接触过了。爱瑞恩知道他将随时出现，如果她需要他。

他重新坐回凯伦旁边的座位。刚坐下就听到扩音器中的声音："女子跳远！"当六个健美苗条的女孩走到跑道上时，他的心又绷紧了。一个女孩脸上的表情很得意，另一个看上去若有所思，但是爱瑞恩一路跛行过来，脸上还是那种常见的自豪而坚定的注视。

爱瑞恩开始热身，而罗伯特从座位上站了起来，像个监护人一样站在那里。凯伦站在他的旁边，"三十分钟过完了吗？"

"我觉得她还没准备好。"罗伯特喃喃地说。

"她生来就准备好一切了。"凯伦信心十足地回答。罗伯特笑了，知道她说的没错。

"爱瑞恩·汤普森上场。"

甚至在裁判宣布之前，罗伯特就知道爱瑞恩跳得不够远。

"13英尺10英寸。"

他为他的女儿感到伤心，但他却没看到她的精神有丝毫颓败。她双手在沙坑上猛捶了几下，然后迅速站了起来，仅用右脚支撑着她纤细的身体。

"加油，爱瑞恩，你能做到的！"罗伯特大喊道，希望她能听到他的声音，能够抬头看看，向他寻求一点支持。可即使爱瑞恩在听，她也不会表现出来。她只是重新又开始舒展身体，为下一次跳远做准备。

这一次她跳的距离更近了，而且这一次爱瑞恩几乎只能爬着走出沙坑。这简直让人难以承受。而她只剩下最后一次机会了。

当其他的参赛者一个个沿着跑道跳出去的时候，罗伯特真希望他能把女儿身上的压力带走，使事情变得好一些。抱抱她，告诉她没事的，无论如何他都爱她。如果她不想再跳了，那也没关系。这只是一场愚蠢的比赛——它其实没什么大不了的。

但他知道它确实很重要。爱瑞恩为它努力了这么久，没有什么能阻止她拼尽全力——即使今天她拼尽全力也无法获奖。

爱瑞恩重重地坐在了黑色的沥青地上，等着她的上场。"只要你看看我，亲爱的。"罗伯特低声乞求着，希望能穿越运动场给她送去些支持。

扩音器刺耳地响了起来："这是你的最后一跳，爱瑞恩·汤普森上场！"

爱瑞恩挣扎着走到了起点，就在起跳之前，她抬头望向了看台。罗伯特读懂了她的意思。她知道他们在守护着她，而她将会竭尽全力。他眨了眨眼睛掩去眼中的潮气，微笑着站在那里，为她加油鼓气。"那是我的女儿，"他大声喊道，"尽力去做吧！"

只要她尽力，对他来说就足够了，他一直都这么觉得。但是对他好强的女儿来说是不是足够呢？最后一次，爱瑞恩沿着跑道出发了，笨拙地朝着她的目标奋进。

"13英尺。"

距离非常短。但这一次，没有双手重重地捶打沙坑。也没有双腿从沙坑中站起。只有一次缓慢的回首，寻找她的父亲，寻求帮助。她需要他。

罗伯特跳过冰冷的黄色护栏，飞奔到了爱瑞恩身边。疼痛的泪水布满了她的双颊。罗伯特跪下身子，轻轻地把她抱起来，带出了沙坑。"我为你自豪，"他在她耳边轻声地说，"你还好吗？"

"当然。我尽全力了，再没有一个女孩能比我做得更好了！"爱瑞恩骄傲地说，虽然罗伯特还能听出她声音中隐藏的疼痛。

"我知道，但我不确定你是否知道。"

"嗨,你这些年都教我什么了?"爱瑞恩说,脸上的表情半是微笑,半是疼痛。

"那是我的女儿,"罗伯特颤抖着说,他的声音泄露了他激动的心情和内心的自豪,"那就是我的女儿。"

·chapter three·

Making a Difference

3

与众不同

Come to Me when you need a pick-me-up, and I'll refresh you and teach you balance. I'm able to make all grace abound to you so that in all things at all times, you'll have all the resources you need to excel in every good work I've planned for you.

Energizing you,
Your God of Power

—from Matthew 11:28–30; 2 Corinthians 9:8

当你需要我时就来到我的身边，我将使你焕然一新，并教你如何平衡。我会把所有美好的东西带到你的身边，并随时供你使用。你将拥有你需要的一切，这将使你胜任我为你准备的一切工作。

充满活力的你，
你力量源泉的上帝

What would happen if you just didn't get out of bed this morning? Oh, maybe that call to the client wouldn't have been made or the closet would still be a mess. But more importantly, would you have been missed?

Have you ever gone on vacation and realized it took four people to do what you do on a normal day? Your friend drove the carpool and took the older kids to baseball practice, your mom picked up your toddler from daycare, your coworker answered your calls and took care of necessary business, and your dad watered your plants and fed your pets. It takes a lot of people to fill in for you.

You are valuable, but not just for those daily chores everyone takes for granted that you'll take care of.

You are valuable for being you.

When you're gone, you're missed because you are a positive force in the lives of those around you. You make your child's day with the little notes you leave in his lunchbox. Your coworkers love to see your smiling face. Your husband needs your encouraging words and a kiss on the cheek after a long day.

That's why you do it. That's why even when life gets tough, or when for whatever reason you're just plain tired, you keep going. You get out of bed, you start your day, and you Ness others with your presence. You hold an important place in their hearts. Because whatever tasks they perform, no one else can be you.

如果今天早晨你起不来会发生什么事情？也许你无法再跟你的客户打电话，或者衣橱里还是始终一片脏乱。但是重要的是，你会不会被思念？

你有没有在普通的一天去度假然后意识到需要四个人来帮忙？你的朋友开车去送你的大儿子练习棒球，你的妈妈从托儿所接来刚会走路的孩子，你的同事帮你接电话以及处理紧急业务，你的爸爸帮你浇灌植物以及喂养宠物。这需要很多人来代替你。

你很重要，并不是因为每个人都保证说你可以完成这些日常家务杂事，你是因你自己而重要。

当你

离开,你会被大家想念。因为在你周围的人的生活中你是他们的积极动力,你在你孩子的午餐盒里留下字条,你的同事喜欢看到你的笑脸,你的丈夫需要一天的劳累得到你的鼓励和面颊上的吻。

　　这就是为什么你这样做,甚至当生活变得艰苦、当不知何故你非常疲惫时,为什么还再坚持下去。起床,开始一天的生活,以你的存在来祝福其他人。在他们的心中你已经占据重要的地位,因为无论他们处于什么样的角色,没有人可以成为你。

Let no man imagine
that he has no influence.
Whoever he may be, and wherever
he may be placed, the man who thinks
becomes a light and a power.

Henry George

任何人都会有他的影响力。不管
他是谁，也不管他在何处，那有着思想
的人会给你光明和力量。

亨利·乔治

*K*im could hardly bring herself to get out of bed.

She never thought this could happen to her.

　　金怎么也无法使自己摆脱床的束缚。

　　她从来就没想到这会发生在她的身上。

Back to School

Kim Matheny's alarm screamed in her ears. Although she knew it was time to get up, the thirty-five-year-old kindergarten teacher lay motionless, head still swimming from the recent turn of events. It had been just seven days since she received the devastating news. She had cancer.

She'd spent the previous week

away from her classroom in a whirlwind of doctor visits, Internet research, and life-or-death decisions. Today was Monday, and she was due back at school. Although she loved her students dearly, she could hardly bring herself to get out of bed, let alone face their questions about why she'd been gone, what was cancer, was she going to die.

Kim forced herself to sit up, knowing she had to keep moving to ward off the looming depression over her diagnosis. She never thought this could happen to her, but reminded herself that no one ever does, and wondered how the kids would handle her illness.

Maybe another teacher would be better for them. No, I'd miss them too much. But what if teaching is more than I can handle right now? I need their cheery faces and sweet hugs. She plopped back down, thoughts racing and panic rising. *What if they've already gotten used to the substitute and don't care if I come back? Kids forget quickly. Maybe I don't matter as much I think—*

"Stop it! " She scolded herself aloud. "Get a grip."

She slammed the snooze button again and let her arm just drop onto the nightstand. Her hand landed on a colorful note she had received the day before.

She picked it up and unfolded it again. The drawing was of a rainbow, a bright yellow sun, and two stick figures. The larger one was labeled "Ms. Matheny" and the smaller one "Me." One figure's arm reached out toward the other's, and the two lines were joined at the bottom with one large, round scribble representing the holding of hands. Then, in purple crayon, "You brighten my day, Ms. Matheny. I miss you. Come back soon." It was signed "Luv, Macy." Tears filled Kim's eyes. *My kids need me.* She got out of bed to get ready for school.

On the drive to Southwood Elementary, Kim thought of numerous ways to greet her class. Her usual song, "It's a beautiful day, it's a beautiful day, the birds are singing, let's shout hooray," didn't seem fitting. The sun was shining and the birds were singing, but she just didn't think she could form those words on her lips today.

The thirty-minute drive and her walk to the

classroom seemed to drift by in a fog. Kim usually was in high gear before class, adjusting the weather chart and setting out the first activity to make sure everything was ready when the students arrived. Today she sat at her desk, perfectly still except for the distracted tapping of her pencil on a stack of papers.

"Hi, Kim." The sympathetic tone belonged to Sarah Richardson, who taught the first-grade class across the hall. "The children will be here shortly. If you need anything today, please come and get me."

Kim looked at her friend nervously. "I don't know if I can do this."

Sarah nodded assurance. "You'll make it. And like I said, I'm here if you need me."

The kind support nearly shattered Kim's resolve not to cry, but she swallowed hard and blinked to clear her eyes. "Thanks."

One by one the children began arriving. Samuel, always eager for school, came running in first. "Ms. Matheny, what are we doing today?" It didn't seem he'd even noticed her weeklong absence.

Kim was disappointed but tried not to let it show. "We have a lot planned for today. I'm so glad you're excited about school," she said with all the enthusiasm she could muster. Her one buoy—the special place she thought she had in her students' hearts—was sinking fast. Had the children even missed her at all?

Nathan arrived next, clutching his mother's pant leg as he used to do. Kim had made such progress with him, but now he treated her like a stranger again.

"He was like this all last week," Nathan's mother said.

"Oh, Nathan." Kim gently rubbed his back, trying to ease her own anxiety as much as his. Had she

lost all the ground she had gained since the beginning of the school year? She just didn't have the heart to start over. "I'm so glad you're here. I sure need my little helper today." Her voice quavered a little, and she stopped, afraid she'd be completely engulfed by discouragement.

Then suddenly Nathan released his mother's leg and turned for his teacher to pick him up.

As Kim hugged him tightly, he whispered, "I´ m so glad you're back."

Next came Sadie. She didn't say a word, but her dimples flashed as she embraced her teacher shyly before scurrying to her desk.

The rest of the class had arrived, but where was Macy? She usually arrived about twenty minutes early to help Kim by setting out scissors or crayons or whatever she asked her to do. Macy hadn't missed a day of school all year. She loved being there and always had a smile to share with a friend. Kim suddenly realized just how much she'd missed Macy's good cheer during the most difficult week of her life. She needed Macy to be there today.

Just as Kim was calling the class to attention, Macy walked into the classroom slowly, with her head down. Not even a hint of the smile Kim so desperately needed. Her spirits sank to a new low. Was Macy not even happy to have her back? Near tears, Kim forced herself to try to sound cheery.

"Well hello, Macy! "

Macy jerked to attention, looking up for the first time since she'd entered the room.

"Ms. Matheny! It's you! " Macy squealed with delight, running to squeeze her teacher's leg as tightly as she could.

"Of course, it's me," Kim giggled, bending to return the hug and thank Macy for her wonderful note.

"I didn't think you were coming back." Macy's eyes were as round and bright as the big yellow sun she had drawn on her picture.

"Yes, Macy, I'm back. I need you little munchkins.

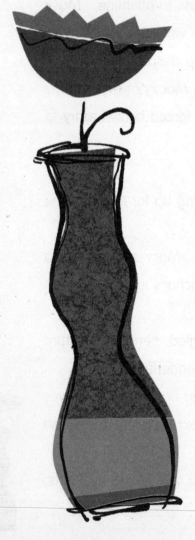

Did you miss me?" Kim asked hopefully.

Macy made a face and answered almost indignantly. "Yes! Who else would teach us to count and write and color?"

"Who'd teach us those silly songs?" another student joined in earnestly.

"Who would tell us who gets to be the line leader or the door holder? That other teacher didn't know anything about that," Samuel added.

"I'm sure your substitute teacher was very good," Kim protested—but not too strongly. She was enjoying this outpouring of affection.

"Not near as good as you,"

Sadie countered.

"Yeah," Macy said adamantly. "And no one can give hugs as good as you! "

At this the entire class ran to the front of the classroom, nearly tackling their beloved teacher as they jostled to get one of her warm hugs and to give one in return.

"Well! " Sarah interrupted from the doorway, smiling approvingly at her friend. "I guess you have everything under control."

Kim laughed. "I don't know about that. But I know this is exactly where I needed to be today. I think we'll be just fine."

"I know you will." Sarah responded confidently.

返回学校

金·玛仕的闹钟在耳边尖叫。尽管这个35岁的幼儿园老师知道该起床了,但她还是一动不动地躺在那里,脑海中翻腾着最近发生的事情,7天前收到令人绝望的信息:她得了癌症。

上周她离开她的班级,用一周的时间旋风般地疯狂看医生、上网查询信息、做生或死的抉择。今天是周一,她知道该去学校了。尽管她很爱她的学生,但她还是不想起来,更不用说能够面对那些关于为什么走了? 什么是癌症? 她会死吗? 等等这些问题。

金强迫自己起来, 她知道自己必须忘掉诊断书上令人忧伤的诊断。她从来没有想到这会发生在自己身上,但是提醒自己其他人也不会这样想的,她在想如何向孩子们交代自己的病?

也许另一个老师对他们会更好。不,那我会非常想念他们。但是如果现在我不能再教他们了怎么办? 我需要他们高兴的笑脸和甜蜜的拥抱。她又躺了下来，思绪万千，痛苦万分。如果他们已经习惯了那个代课老师，不再关心我是否回来该怎么办？孩子都是很快忘记一切的。也许我不应该在意我所想的这些。

"别再胡思乱想了，控制一下自己。"她大声责备自己。她按了一下闹钟上的打盹按钮，胳膊垂在床头，她的手碰到了几天前收到的色彩鲜艳的留言条。

她捡起来然后再次打开。上面画着彩虹，明亮的黄太阳以及两个呆头呆脑的人，个子高的旁边标着"金女士"，个子矮的标着"我"，一个人的胳膊伸向一个人，两条交叉的线画在下面代表紧紧握着彼此的手。然后旁边用紫色蜡笔写道："金女士，您照亮了我的世界，我很想念您，快点回来吧。"署名"鲁·玛西"。看到这些，眼泪充满了金的双眼。我的孩子们需要我。她立刻起床准备去学校。

在开车前往楠木小学的路上，金想了很多方式跟孩子们打招呼。她以前经常唱起一首歌："这是美好的一天，这是美好的一天，小鸟在歌唱，让我们一起欢乐地歌唱。"看来今天是不适合了，阳光是很灿烂，小鸟也在唱歌，但是今天她觉得自己无法从嘴里唱出这些歌词。

半小时的路程以及走在去教室的路上都感觉自己是在雾里飘荡。平时课前她总是激情高涨，校正天气预报图，当孩子到来时着手做第一个活动确保所有的事情准备完毕。那天她坐在桌旁，除了不停地用铅笔在一堆纸上乱敲之外，一切还是很好的。

与众不同

教一年级的萨拉·理查森来到讲堂前,同情地说:"嗨,金,孩子们马上就要到了,如果今天有什么需要帮忙的,就来找我。"

金紧张地看着她的朋友:"我不知道我还能不能讲课。"

萨拉很坚信地点了点头:"你可以的,我说了,如果有什么需要,我一直就在你的身边。"

这种鼓励差点动摇她打算不再流泪的决心,但她还是眨了眨眼努力抑制住泪水。"谢谢你。"

孩子们陆续到了,热切渴望上学的萨姆尔总是第一个跑着到教室,"老师,我们今天都上什么啊?"看上去他并没有注意到老师已经一周没有来上课了。

金很失望,但是没有表现出来。她怀着她所有的激情说:"我们今天有新的计划,我很高兴你对学习有如此高的积极性。"她的唯一精神支柱——以为在孩子的心中有特殊的地位——正在迅速地消失,难道孩子们真的对她一点点思念都没有吗?

下一个来的是内森,他还是那样,紧紧地抓住妈妈的裤腿。金曾经让他进步很多,但是现在他再次对她非常陌生。

"上周他一直都是这样。"内森的妈妈说。

"哦,内森。"金温柔地抚摩他的背,试图放松彼此的担忧情绪,难道这一年来自己树立的威信渐渐消失了吗?她还没有做好失去这一切的思想准备。"很高兴你来了,我今天特别需要帮助的小助手。"她的声音有点颤抖,然后她停了下来,害怕自己淹没在无边的沮丧中。

突然内森放开妈妈的腿,转身跑向他的老师让她抱起来。

当金紧紧抱住他时,他在她的耳边悄悄地说:"我很高兴你能回来。"

下一个是赛蒂,她什么也没有说,但在赶向课桌前拥抱老师时露出羞涩的酒窝。

其他的孩子都到了,但是玛西呢?平时她总是提前20分钟到校,帮助老师摆好剪刀或蜡笔或其他老师让她做的事情,她一年来从没有缺过一次课。她喜欢这里并且总是微笑面对小伙伴们。金突然意识到,在自己一生中最难过的那周里,自己是如何想念玛西的笑脸,今天她尤其需要玛西在她身边。

当金正准备喊起立的时候,玛西低着头慢慢走进教室,没有一丝金迫切需要看到的笑容,金的心情彻底落到了最低点。难道玛西不高兴她回来吗?金快要落下眼泪,但她还是迫使自己高兴地打招呼:"你好吗?玛西!"

玛西突然间意识到什么,自从进教室以来第一次抬起头来。"金,是你!"玛西高兴地尖叫起来,快速跑到老师面前,紧紧抱住老师的腿。

"当然是我。"金开心地笑起来,弯下身抱住她,感谢她送给她最棒的留言条。

"我没有想到你回来了。"玛西的眼睛正如她的画里的太阳一样又大又明亮。

"是的,我回来了,我很需要你,你想念我吗?"金抱着极大的

希望问道。

玛西做了个鬼脸，几乎愤慨地回答："是啊！还有谁像您一样教我们数数、写字和涂色彩？"

另一个学生也急切地说："还有谁可以教我们那些傻傻的歌曲？"

撒姆尔补充说："谁可以告诉我们将来谁可以成为排长或者门卫？其他老师根本不懂这些。"

"我确信代课老师是非常棒的，"金提出异议——但是并不是那么强烈。她非常享受这种感情的宣泄。

"但是没有你好，"夏蒂反对。

玛西非常坚定地说："是的，没有人像您这么好可以给我们拥抱！"

在这个时候，全班的学生都跑到教室前方，他们拥挤着得到老师温暖的拥抱，然后让给下一个同学，他们这样轮流着差点挤倒他们深爱的老师。

"哇！"萨拉从门口进来打断了他们，赞许地笑着对自己的朋友说："我猜你已经处理好所有的事情。"

金大笑着说："我不知道，但是今天我已经确切地知道了哪里最需要我，我认为我们将会变得更好。"

"我知道你肯定会的。"萨拉很自信地回应。

·chapter four·

Cherishing Old Friend

4

珍视老朋友

I've called you My friend.
I've chosen you and
appointed you to make a
lasting difference. Loving
each other is what counts!
Friends love at all times
and help each other in the
hard times.

Loving you always,
Your Friend and King
—from John 15:15–17; Proverbs 17:17

　　我拜访了你，我的朋友。我选择了你，并使你成为永久的不变。相互的爱是十分重要的！朋友之间要永远相爱，尤其是在艰难的时刻。

　　永远地爱你，
　你的朋友以及金

"*Make new friends* but keep the old.   One is silver and the other gold." It's an old song, but it rings even more true today than when you first learned it. Now you understand it.

It's great to make new friends,   but friendships that have withstood the test of time are priceless. There's nothing better than having a friend who was in the waiting room when you delivered your first baby and then again when your husband was in the ICU.

Someone who really listens when you need to talk,   who will meet you at the mall when you need a break from your daily routine,   who doesn't notice if your house is a mess when she drops by to say hello.

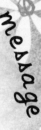

Jesus said, "Greater love has no one than this, that he lay down his life for his friends" (John 15:13). Wow. That's a friend indeed.

Most of us don't have occasion to literally lay down our lives for our friends. But we can lay down our lives every day, in a million little ways. We can break through our self-protection to share life's deepest struggles and joys. We can sacrifice the "important" things we had to do today to spend time with a friend who's lonely. We can take a few minutes to write a note or give a hug to a friend who's done such things for us.

Old friends, like gold, are treasures. Let them know they're cherished.

"结交新朋友,联系老朋友。新朋友是银,

老朋友是金。"这是一首老歌中的歌词。如今听起来比

第一次听时更加有道理。因为现在你理解了它的含义。

　　结交新朋友是件好事，但经过时间考验的友谊尤其

珍贵。没有什么比当你产下第一个婴儿,有人在诊室外

面等候你更好的了;没有什么比当你丈夫在重症病房

也有朋友在外等候你更好的了。你想说话有朋友

愿意倾听,你想调整日常的生活放松一下,

有朋友在商场门口等你。朋友来家小

坐时并不介意你家中的凌乱。

耶稣说:"人为朋

友舍命,人的

爱心

没有比这个更大的。"（约翰15:13）哇，
这才是真正的朋友。

大多数人并不会遇到真正要为朋友舍命的场合，但
我们每天都可以用各种不同的方式为朋友做事。我们可
以打破自我保护，分享生活的酸甜苦辣。我们可以牺牲
今天必须做的"重要"事情，陪伴一位孤独的朋友。
我们也可以花几分钟时间给为你做以上事情的
朋友写个便条或拥抱他一下。

老朋友就像金子一样弥足珍
贵。要让他们知道我们很珍
惜他们。

That best portion of a good man's life,
[are] His little nameless
unremembered acts of kindness
and love.

William Wordsworth

一个好人生命中最好的部分
是他无名的永刻在人们心中的仁
爱之心。

威廉·伍滋沃斯

Charles knew he was disappointing his friends, but it wasn't just the arthritis holding him back.

查尔斯知道他让他的朋友们失望，但这不是他的关节炎在阻碍他。

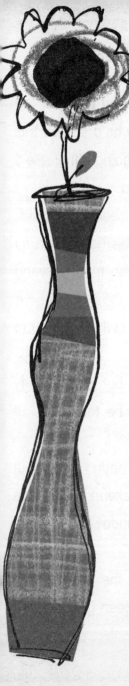

Fore!

"I'm not sure if I'm going to make it this year." Charles grimaced as he said this into the phone. He knew it wouldn't be taken well.

"What are you talking about?" David responded. "It's a tradition, Charles, you have to be there."

Charles didn't know how he was going to handle being at home on this third weekend in July, the weekend his three closest friends would be at the Iron Horse Golf Course in Texas just as they had been for the past fifty-four years. He was the one who'd started this tradition. But he simply couldn't handle going either. He'd thought about it a lot. This would be best.

"David, you know how much I love seeing you guys, but I just can't play anymore. My arthritis has gotten so bad that I'd be in bed for a week if I even tried to swing a club."

"So come and just ride in the cart. We want you to be there."

"I'lle think about it," Charles said, but he'd already made up his mind that the trip would be too hard. It Wasn't just the arthritis holding him back.

Mary had died in January, and he hadn't gotten out much since then. This year the third weekend in July was not only the golf reunion date; that Sunday would have been his and Mary's anniversary.

The tradition had gotten its start the weekend of their wedding. Each of these guys had been groomsmen, and they played golf the day before the ceremony. They'd come back every year since.

This had drawn a few complaints from Mary over the years, when the calendar rotation meant he was gone on their anniversary. But she never really minded. She knew how much his friends meant to him, and they always made sure to take a trip or do something special together the weekend before.

"Well, I don't know what we are going to do without you," Dave said. "It just won't be the same." They said their good-byes.

"Edwin, can you believe he's not coming?" David said into the phone. He had immediately dialed Edwin's number after talking with Charles. He knew Edwin would have a solution. He'd always been the leader of the group, which was probably precisely why Charles had not broken the news to him. *Edwin wouldn't have let him off the hook so easily,* David thought, kicking himself for not saying the right thing.

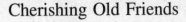

Cherishing Old Friends

The two friends agreed that this had to be a rough year for Charles, and they understood his grief at his first anniversary without his wife. But it seemed to them the worst thing he could do was stay at home, alone. They wanted to be there to support him during this time. That's what friends were for, after all. But just how were they going to convince Charles to join them?

"I can't believe he used the arthritis as an excuse," Edwin said. "He should know I'll never let him get away with that. Remember the year I broke my leg and still came, cast and all?"

David laughed and cringed. "Yeah, you nearly broke your other leg trying to swing a club while balancing on the one good leg! "

Edwin chuckled, then sighed. "I'll call John. He's been through this. It's only been three years since Lisa passed away, maybe he can encourage Charles and convince him to come."

"He is not changing his mind," John told Edwin a week later, after many phone calls between the four friends. "I've tried everything, and I can't convince him. He's afraid he'll be too sad, between thoughts of Mary and being stuck riding in the cart, unable to play. Said he'd just bring us all down and none of us would have any fun."

"Well, that beats all," Edwin said. There was a pause, then he continued decisively. "I won't have it. We can't let him sit at home because he's worried about ruining the trip for us. We'll just have to go get him."

"That would be the only way to get him there," John agreed, not sure if his friend was serious.

"I mean it, John. We'll show up at his doorstep and

drag him to the course." Edwin had spoken. Their course was set.

"This won't be easy since he lives at least three states away from any of us." John grinned, knowing full well Edwin would pull it off even though their work and families had spread them each to a different part of the country.

"This is not a good day for company," Charles grumbled as the doorbell rang again.

He hadn't gotten any sleep the night before, tossing and turning with grief for his wife and regret at his decision to stay home on this weekend. He knew he was disappointing his friends. They had all come in for the funeral, and it had meant the world to him. Maybe he should go. He hadn't booked a plane ticket though, so it really was out of the question.

I could just get in the car and start driving, he thought. It was Thursday afternoon, and Charles had been thinking about that option all morning. His friends

would all be flying into town on Friday. He could make it if he started driving by dinnertime.

Or maybe he had made the right decision. He'd be terrible company like this. They counted on him to keep everyone laughing. He'd always been the fun guy. But not this year. He didn't want his friends to see him like this. Maybe after he got past the hurdle of this first year. Maybe he'd be back next year.

Charles's mind was still in turmoil as he shuffled reluctantly to the door and opened it.

"FORE! " Edwin, David, and John shouted in unison.

Charles just stood there, mouth agape, as his friends all began talking at once, each saying how much their longtime friend meant to them and vowing not to leave until he had packed his bags and agreed to come along.

"Oh yeah," Edwin said. "And can we take your car?"

They all burst into laughter, and Charles was glad to have an excuse for the moistening in his eyes.

Cherishing Old Friends

"It'll be a road trip, just like in our college days," Edwin said with a twinkle in his eyes. "We'll even stop to buy you those pink snowball things you always liked to eat."

"How can I say no to snowballs?" Charles said, all hesitation gone. "I'll go pack my bags."

"Get your clubs too," David shouted after him. "Yours are a lot better than mine, and if you're just going to be sitting in the cart, I might as well put them to good use."

Charles returned with a small duffel bag of clothes, his golf bag, and tears in his eyes. He'd decided there was no use trying to hide anything from such good friends. "Thanks, guys. You'll never know how much I needed you to walk through that door when you did."

"That's what friends are for," Edwin said, slapping him gently on the back. "That's what friends are for."

领军人物

"我不能肯定今年是否能参加。"查尔斯对着电话说这句话时面露苦相。他知道这件事有点难。

"你说什么呢？"大卫回答道。"每年都是这样，查尔斯，你必须去那儿。"

7月的第3个周末，查尔斯的3个好朋友要去得克萨斯州参加铁马高尔夫比赛，像过去的54年一样；而他却待在家里，他不知道如何在家打发时间。他是第一个开始这么做的，但现在他却无法参加。他考虑了很久，待在家里可能是最好的选择。

"大卫，你知道我是多么想见到你们几个，但是我却打不了高尔夫了。我的关节炎越来越厉害了，哪怕是只挥一杆，我都得卧床休息一周。"

"所以还是来吧，哪怕就坐在手推车上，我们只想看见你在那儿。"

"让我想想吧，"查尔斯说，但他知道来回的路程对他来说太艰难了。但关节炎并不是唯一的原因。

1月，玛丽去世离开了他，他还没有完全从悲痛的阴影中走出来。今年7月的第3个周末不仅是和朋友打高尔夫相聚的日子，那个周日还是他和玛丽的结婚纪念日。

他们举行婚礼的那个周末，大家就开始了这种聚会。他们都是伴郎，婚礼前一天他们就开始一起打高尔夫了。从那以后，每年他们都要回来。

那几年，每当查尔斯要去和朋友聚会时，玛丽就会发发牢骚。但她并不是当真的。她知道朋友对他来说意味着什么，在他们结婚纪念日的前一周，他们总是一起旅行或是做一件特别的事情。

"嗯，我真不知道没有你我们会怎样，"大卫说。"没有你就是和以前不一样。"他们和他告别时说。

"埃得温，你相信他不来吗？"大卫对着电话话筒问。他和查尔斯一打完电话就拨通了埃得温的号码。他知道埃得温会有办法解决这件事的。埃得温是他们的头儿，这也可能是查尔斯没有和他中断联系的主要原因。大卫想，埃得温不会让查尔斯这么轻易地离开他们，不给一个恰当的理由就自动放弃的。

两个人一致认为，今年对于查尔斯来说不好过，他们理解他的悲伤：第一个结婚纪念日还没到，妻子就去世了。但是对于他们来说，最糟糕的事情却是查尔斯独自一人待在家里。他们想陪伴他、安慰他。这才是朋友应该做的。但他们又如何能够说服查尔斯加入他们呢？

"我不相信他用关节炎做借口，"埃得温说。"他应该知道我不会就这么轻易放过他的。还记得有一年我的腿摔断了，但还是来参加了？"

大卫笑了，似乎还心有余悸。"对，那次你为了能击一杆球，只能用那只好腿保持平衡，差点儿把那条腿也弄断了！"

埃得温抿着嘴笑了，然后又叹了一口气。"我给约翰打电话。他也经历过同样的痛苦。莉萨去世已经3年了，也许他能说服查尔斯来。"

"他不愿意改变主意，"一周之后约翰告诉埃得温，4个朋友之间通了许多次电话。"我已经尽力了，但我无法说服他。他担心坐在手推车上，自己又不能玩，想玛丽时会伤心过度。那样我们所有的人都被他弄得情绪低落，谁都不会开心。"

"那就糟了，"埃得温说。稍微停顿了一会儿，接着他又果断地说，"我不会让他这样的。正因为他担心坏了我们的好事，我们才不能让他一个人待在家里。我们应该去接他来。"

"对，这才是唯一的办法，"约翰同意埃得温的想法，却不确定他是否是认真的。

"我是当真的，约翰。我们会出现在他家门口，然后把他拽过来。"埃得温说。他们就这么决定了。

"但这事并不容易,因为他离我们3个当中的任何一个人都至少有3个州的距离。"约翰咧咧嘴,他知道埃得温会做到的,哪怕工作和家庭将他们每一个人分散在不同的地方。

"这可不是一个来客人的好日子,"门铃再次响起的时候,查尔斯嘟囔着说。

从前天夜里开始,他就没有睡好觉,思念妻子,后悔这个周末待在家里的决定。当时他们几个全都来参加葬礼了,这对他来说很重要。也许这个周末他真应该去。他还没订机票,因此不可能去了。

我应该上车,然后启动,他想。周四查尔斯一上午都在想这个问题。周五他的朋友们都会坐飞机去的。如果他晚饭前发动车子还能来得及。

也许他的决定是正确的。他想这样有点可怕。他们还指望他逗他们笑呢。他一直就是一个爱找乐子的人。但今年不是。他不想让朋友们看到他这样。也许他能渡过今年这个难关。也许明年他还会回去。

查尔斯不情愿地向门口走去,开门时脑中仍然一片混乱。

"Fore!"埃得温、大卫和约翰一同叫道。查尔斯愣愣地站在那儿,瞠目结舌。他们3个开始说话了,每个人都说查尔斯对他们来说很重要,并说除非他收拾东西同意和他们一起走,否则绝不离开。

"哦,耶,"埃得温说,"我们能坐你的车吗?"

大家全都笑了起来,查尔斯双眼湿润,在朋友面前什么也无所谓了。

"这是一次汽车旅行，就像我们上大学时那样。"埃得温说着，眨了眨眼睛。"我们甚至可以停车，下去给你买那些平时你最爱吃的粉红色的'雪球'一类的食物。"

"我怎么能对'雪球'说不呢？"查尔斯说，他再也不犹豫了。"我马上收拾东西。"

"把你的球杆也带着。"大卫在他身后叫道。"你的球杆比我的好，当你坐在手推车上休息时，我也能让它们发挥作用。"

查尔斯回来时，已经收拾好一包衣服和高尔夫球包，眼睛里闪烁着泪花。他发现在这些好朋友面前，没有必要掩饰任何情感。"谢谢你们。你们不知道我多么希望你们能走进那扇门，刚才你们都做到了。"

"那才是朋友应该做的，"埃得温边说边在他背上轻轻地拍了一下。"那才是朋友应该做的。"

Enjoying

Surprises

•chapter five•

Enjoying Surprises

5

享受惊喜

Experience My abundant life! I'm continuing to work behind the scenes on your behalf, and I love to far exceed your expectations and dreams. Taste and see My goodness in your life.

Blessing you,
Your God of Wonder

—from John 10:10; Ephesians 3:20, Psalm 34:8

经历我无穷无尽的生命，我将继续站在你的背后，为你鼓劲，我热爱你远大的期望和梦想。体验并观察我在你生命中的仁爱。

保佑你，你的

令人惊讶的上帝

Surprise! Have you ever heard that word shouted by a large group of friends and family? It's so much fun! Kids young and old love a surprise party. Everyone comes abuzz with anticipation, chattering about how they almost slipped and gave away the secret or wondering if the surprise suspects anything.

Perhaps the only feeling more exciting than receiving such a surprise is perpetrating one. Planning a big surprise makes you feel great, doesn't it? You can't help but tingle with excitement. In fact, you realize, you've smiled more in the days leading up to the event than you have all year!

Sure, some people aren't comfortable with parties, but don't believe it when they tell you they don't like surprises. Whatever form it takes, we all like to have something special done for us. Something thoughtful, be it big or small, that we didn't have to lift a finger for and that we never expected.

Why are surprises so great? Because when someone surprises you with a party, a single flower on your desk,or a sparkling clean house, it means that someone thought of you, cared about your happiness so much that he or she did something just for you.

If you haven't surprised anyone lately, even with something little, it's time. Choose someone you love, put in a little thought and planning, and just do it. You'll both be surprised at how good it feels.

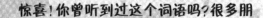

　　惊喜!你曾听到过这个词语吗?很多朋友和家庭都有这样的感叹。它给人们带来很多快乐。孩子们和老年人喜欢这样给人惊喜的聚会。人们热热闹闹地聚在一起,都期望获得惊喜,叙述他们如何差点摔倒,如何把自己知道的秘密告诉别人。

　　也许,得到这些惊喜给人的感觉更多的是一些胡说八道的事。编造一个让人惊喜的故事使人感觉很了不起,难道不是吗?你忍不住感到惊讶。事实上,惊喜的事件使你在整个一年中都感到很快乐。

　　确实,有些人在人群中感到不舒服,但当他们说他们不喜欢惊喜,你可不要相信。不管惊喜以什么形式出现,人们

都喜欢做某些特别的事情。这些惊喜

　是想得很周到，也许是很大的，也许很小，这些惊喜

不需要我们花费很大的力气，或从来就不曾指望的。

　　为什么惊喜有如此大的力量？因为当某人在聚会时

在你的桌上放一枝花，或把房间装饰得闪闪发光，这说

明别人想着你，关心你的幸福，而为你特别制造的这

份惊喜。

　　如果你还没为别人制造过什么惊喜，哪怕

是很小的惊喜，那只是时间的问题。你会选

择你所爱的人，为他或她想想并做出

计划，给出你的惊喜。你会为给

别人惊喜而感觉很好。

Into all our lives, in many simple, familiar, homely ways, God infuses this element of joy from the surprises of life, which unexpectedly brighten our days and fill our eyes with light.

Samuel Longfellow

上帝把快乐灌注在我们的生活中，使得我们这些凡夫俗子熟知的普通家庭生活充满着惊奇，这使得我们的生活更加亮丽，使得我们眼前一片光明。

萨矛尔

Cynthia had been longing for a romantic getaway. Going fishing wasn't Hawaii, but it was something.

莎斯亚一直期盼着有个浪漫的私奔，到夏威夷钓鱼不是目的，而是为了别的。

The Fishing Trip

"Thank you so much, Kathy, for taking care of the kids today," Cynthia said as she and Tom dropped off their children at her best friend's house.

"No problem. You two have a good time," Kathy responded, shooing the couple out the door.

"Bye, darlings. You be sweet. We'll be back after dinner."

Enjoying Surprises

Cynthia gave each child a kiss on of the head. The children giggled and hugged their mom tightly.

"Kathy seems almost as excited about our anniversary as we are! " Cynthia remarked as they walked back to the car.

Four children between the ages of eight and two didn't leave Tom and Cynthia much time alone together, but today was their tenth anniversary, and they were going to the lake and then out to dinner. Cynthia had hoped for more, but this would be nice, and she had resigned herself to the fact that this was all they could do.

Off and on throughout the year, Cynthia had been thinking back to their honeymoon. It had been a dream-vacation to Hawaii, and they had stayed at a beautiful resort—before dirty diapers and middle-of-the-night feedings took over. That was the last time she and Tom had taken a trip together, and she wanted so badly to do something really special for their tenth anniversary.

She wasn't complaining, really. She enjoyed their full life. They'd both wanted a house full of children, and it didn't take long before they had gotten their wish. A family that large, though, did pose some challenges. Just planning a "date night" every once in a while was a task, much less actually going away for a weekend. Anyway, by the time they got four kids through diapers, formula, doctor visits, and piano lessons, the extra money for a vacation was just never there.

Still, ever since their youngest child was weaned off the bottle, Cynthia had keen longing for a getaway. She was ready to put some focus back on her and Tom again, to do something fun and exciting that didn't involve kids. She'd dropped several hints about how great it would be to recapture those romantic moments from their honeymoon, to actually sleep with just the two of them in the bed without one or two little bodies sneaking in during the middle of the night.

Cynthia had even gathered information on cruises and trips to the beach and left them lying around for Tom to see. But they couldn't do it, Tom had told her. They just didn't have the extra funds.

"You're right," she had said with a sigh. "Besides, what would we do with the kids? It would be a nightmare trying to find someone to keep them. And ugh," she'd gone on, trying to be a good sport, "just the thought of packing for all of them! "

So they had decided to go fishing. It wasn't Hawaii, but it was something she and Tom had loved doing together when they were dating and newly married. They still took the kids fishing fairly often, but it was always a major effort to get them all packed up. Then they spent most of their time putting fresh bait on each child's hook after the fish had nibbled it away without ever biting into the hook. Cynthia was looking forward to this more relaxed outing.

"This will be fun," she said with a smile, leaning over in the suburban to give her husband a kiss on the cheek as they pulled out of her friend's driveway.

Tom seemed glad for the break too. "Yeah, it's just you and me, baby. Are you sure you're OK with the fact that we didn't get to go on that dream vacation?"

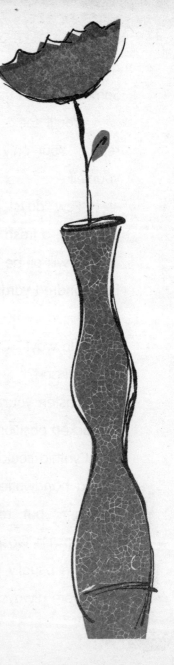

"Oh, sure. Just spending the day with you will be great," she reassured him. "But for our twentieth anniversary, I'm expecting no less than the Bahamas! "

Tom laughed. "All right, I promise."

"Where do you want to eat tonight ? " Cynthia asked absentmindedly as she settled back to enjoy the ride.

"Oh, I don't care. You might want to wait and decide that when we get there."

Cynthia thought she caught a bit of mischief in his tone. It was the way he used to sound when he had a fun secret. "When we get where?" she asked, sitting up straight. Tom broke into a full grin. Something was up.

"You'll see," he replied teasingly. "Just sit back and relax. Your only job for the next few days is to enjoy yourself."

"Few days! Did you say *few days*?" Cynthia squealed, a fresh sparkle in her eyes.

"It will all be clear soon enough," he insisted. Just a few hundred yards later, he took the exit ramp that read Airport.

"No way! " Cynthia exclaimed. "Really, are we going to the airport?"

"Fasten your safety belt and put your tray tables in the locked position," Tom joked, passing her a note.

Cynthia couldn't unfold the paper fast enough. On it was a handwritten poem. Tom had written her many poems, but recently they'd become few and far between. He wasn't very good at poetry, to be honest— his were usually pretty corny. But Cynthia didn't care. They were always funny and warm, and she had saved

The Fishing Trip

every one. She read aloud:

To my wife of ten amazing years,

I love you more each day.

That's why I wanted to surprise you

In this very special way.

Today I hope to fulfill your dream

And fill your heart with joy;

I'm taking you on a trip to Cancun,

Now come here and kiss this boy!

It's you and me, babe, for five nights and days,

To do whatever we wish:

Take walks on the beach or naps in our room,

Who knows—we might even fish.

The kids are in good hands,

You're mom's on her way.

You're bag is packed, our room is booked,

So let's go! What do you say?

Cynthia brushed away a tear and laughed. She suddenly felt lighter than air. "I say you're the greatest husband in the whole world! " She nearly caused a fender–

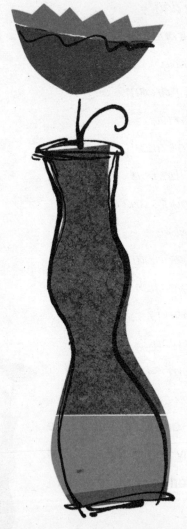

bender smothering Tom with kisses as he pulled into a parking space at the airport.

She couldn't stop smiling as she got out of the car. As she walked toward the back of the vehicle, she saw Tom unloading their suitcases, which had been hidden under a blanket behind the backseat. "Oh, no, how in the world did you know what to pack?"

"Kathy came over yesterday while you took Aaron to baseball practice. If we forgot anything, I guess we'll just have to buy it there."

"Did you happen to forget my swimsuit? I could use a new one," Cynthia said with a sly grin.

Tom smiled back. "You can

buy whatever you want. I've been saving for this trip for a while now."

Cynthia was stunned. "OK, I've always thought you were the greatest husband—now I know you are! " She gave him a long kiss.

As they walked up to the ticket counter hand in hand, pulling their luggage behind them, Cynthia was reminded again of what had made her fall in love with Tom in the first place. He made the little things, the day-to-day stuff, seem special—and the big things absolutely wonderful. He must have worked hard to plan this little surprise. She was looking forward to hearing her mom and the kids and Kathy tell all about how they had kept the big secret and pulled this off. But for now, at last, it was just the two of them heading off to a "fishing trip" she knew she'd never forget.

带你去旅行

"凯西,今天你帮我们照看孩子,实在非常感谢。"和汤姆一起把孩子送到好朋友家时,辛西娅对凯西说。

"放心吧,你们俩就好好享受二人世界吧!",说着,凯西把他们俩送出门。

"亲爱的,跟妈妈再见。你们要乖一点,爸爸妈妈吃完晚饭就来接你们。"辛西娅亲吻了每个小家伙的额头,孩子们也都咯咯笑着紧紧抱住妈妈。

"对于咱们的纪念日,凯西好像也同样兴奋。"去拿车时,辛西娅对丈夫说。

有4个2~8岁的孩子需要照料,辛西娅和汤姆很少有时间单独相处。但今天是他们结婚十周年纪念日,他们要一起去湖边钓鱼,然后共进晚餐。对于这个特殊的日子,辛西娅其实有更多的期待,但是就这样度过,她也满意了,她知道能这样已经很不容易了。

这些年,辛西娅时常会想起他们度蜜月时的情景。那时,他们去了梦寐以求的夏威夷,住在一个风景美丽的地方。而那之后的生活就完全被洗尿布、半夜起来喂孩子这样的琐事所取代。那次夏威夷之旅是他们最后一次一起旅行,辛西娅急切渴望能以一种非常特别的方式来度过他们的10周年纪念。

辛西娅不是抱怨,真的不是。她对现在的生活很满意。她和汤姆都想多要几个孩子,家里热热闹闹。结婚不久,他们的愿望就实现了。但是这样一个大家庭着实也有很多挑战。夫妻偶尔抽空来一次"约会"都很难,更不要说单独出去过周末。况且,在支付了4个孩子的尿布、奶粉、看病吃药、学琴等费用之后,哪还有余钱去旅行呀。

但是自从最小的孩子断奶之后,辛西娅就一直期盼着能有一次短暂的解脱。她要把心思更多地用在自己和汤姆身上,和他一起去做一些有趣而又令人兴奋的事,没有孩子的叨扰。她曾好几次暗示丈夫,重新体味蜜月时的浪漫时刻,两个人静静躺着,不用担心会有一两个小家伙半夜偷偷挤进中间,该有多幸福。

辛西娅也曾收集过去海边旅行的信息,然后把它放在汤姆可以看见的地方。可是汤姆对她说,因为没有足够的钱,所以他们还不能去。

"你说得对",她叹口气。"再说了,孩子怎么办?要找个人照看他们实在太难了。哎,"她继续说道,尽量让自己听起来不那么

伤感，"光是想想给他们收拾出发的行装就很可怕了。"

于是他们决定去钓鱼。虽然没有夏威夷那么令人向往，但那也曾经是他们约会、新婚时很喜欢做的事情。平时，他们也经常带着孩子们去钓鱼，可是光是给他们准备行装就够两口子忙一阵的。然后就是不断给孩子的渔竿上换鱼饵，因为鱼儿们总能不咬到鱼钩就从孩子们的渔竿上把诱饵叼走。因此，对于这次轻松的二人钓，辛西娅非常期盼。

"一定会很好玩。"她笑着说。车离开朋友家时，她偷偷把头歪过去轻轻吻了一下丈夫的脸庞。

汤姆看起来也很愉快。"一定会的。只有你和我。宝贝儿，不能带你去梦寐以求的夏威夷，你真的没有不高兴吗？"

"当然不会了。这样特别的日子只要有你陪在身边，我就很满足了。"她尽力不让丈夫感到歉疚。"但是到我们结婚20周年纪念日的时候，我可一定要去巴哈马群岛哦。"

汤姆笑起来，"好，我保证。"

"今天晚饭你想去哪里吃饭？"辛西娅随意问道，她靠着座位，享受着惬意的旅程。

"我嘛，没关系啦。等到了地方，由你来决定。"

从丈夫的口气中辛西娅感觉到了一丝掩藏不住的兴奋。而这种口气只是当他有什么小秘密的时候才会有。"等到了地方？什么地方呀？"她一下子坐直了，急切地问道。汤姆咧嘴大笑，看来有事情要发生了。

"你会知道的，"他笑着说。"做好了，轻松一些。接下来几天你要做的就是好好享受。"

"几天？你是说几天时间？"辛西娅大声问道，眼里闪过兴奋的喜悦。

"你很快就都知道了。"他还是忍着不说。又开了几百码的距离，车子驶上了去机场的路。

"不会吧！"辛西娅尖叫起来。"是真的吗？我们真的是去机场吗？"

"记得系好安全带，把放餐盘的小桌子固定好。"汤姆开玩笑说，递给她一张纸条。

辛西娅迫不及待打开纸条。上面是一首手写的诗。汤姆曾经为她写过很多首诗，但是最近几年越来越少了。说实话，他并不擅长写诗，他写的都不过是些温馨甜蜜老套的句子。但辛西娅并不在乎。她觉得这些诗很有趣，很温暖，每一首她都保存着。她大声读起来。

写给我的爱人

10年了

我一天比一天更爱你

今天我要给你一份惊喜

以这种特别的方式

今天我要让你梦想成真

让你的心中充满喜悦

享受惊喜

我要带你去美丽的坎昆岛

来吧,亲爱的

亲亲旁边这个爱你的人

宝贝,5天5夜的时间

只有你和我

尽情地享受这难得的时光

在沙滩散步

在房中午休

或许———我们还会钓鱼

孩子们已经安排妥当

我的爱人你也已经在路上了

行李整理好了,房间也预定了

宝贝

我们出发

好吗

  抹去激动的泪滴,辛西娅露出甜蜜的笑容。她突然觉得整个人就要幸福地飘起来了。"你是世界上最棒的丈夫。"她热烈地亲吻丈夫,这让正在忙于停车的汤姆差点撞到机场停车位旁边的护栏。

  下了车,她还是兴奋地微笑着。走到车后面,她看见汤姆拿出了用毯子盖着藏在后座下面的行李箱。"噢,天哪,你知道都该带些什么东西吗？"

"昨天你带艾伦去练习棒球时,凯西过来帮忙收拾的。如果有什么东西忘了的,就到了再买吧。"

"那你是不是刚好也忘了带我的泳衣了？我要买一件新的。"辛西娅调皮地笑着。

看着她,汤姆也笑着说,"你想买什么都可以。为了这次旅行我已经攒了很久钱了。"

辛西娅有些惊讶。"我一直觉得你是最好的丈夫——现在我知道你就是。"她深情地长吻汤姆。

他们手牵着手向售票柜台走去,身后拖着行李。这一幕又让辛西娅想起了自己当初是怎样爱上汤姆的。他总是能把那些很小的事情、很普通的细节变得特别——而大事就做到几乎完美。为了安排这次小小的惊喜,他一定工作得很辛苦。她盼望着听母亲、孩子和凯西告诉她,他们是怎样保守这个秘密,不让她知道的。但是现在,这个时候,就只有他们两个人出发去"钓鱼",她知道这次旅行她将永生难忘。

Believing

the Best

·chapter six·

Believing the Best

6

相信最好的

You can always count on Me to fulfill all of My promises to you. My faithfulness is guaranteed. I'm always for you! Nothing can ever separate you from My love.

Hugs,
Your Promise Keeper

—from Psalms 145:13; 100:5; Romans 8:31, 38–39

　　你可以永远得到我，去完成我希望你完成的一切。我的真诚是有保证的。我为你到永远！什么也无法把你我分开。

　　　　拥抱，你希望的保证者

"You can't do that!" "There's no way! " "Just forget it! " "You're way too busy! " Ever heard those objections? Unfortunately, sometimes they come from inside our own heads.

Some people, though, never seem to let those thoughts cross their minds. They're the ones who say there's no such thing as "can't." And they seem to have all the fun. They take skydiving lessons, go on safaris in the jungles of Africa,or invent solutions to "unsolvable" problems.

They aren't rich, necessarily—not just the beautiful people or the smartest or the most talented. Their secret isn't what they have or do or are. It's how they think.

They believe.

They believe they can do anything they put their minds to and that nothing will happen to them that they can't rise above.

They believe worry is wasteful and know that if they just keep going, things will work out in the end.

And they believe persevering through trials develops strength and endurance, empowering them for the next great adventure—or the next challenge.

What separates these can-do people who live fulfilling, fantastic lives from the rest of us? Nothing, really, if you just believe.

"你不能那样做！""没门！""忘了它吧！""多此一举！"这些拒辞是否耳熟呢？遗憾的是，有时候你也是这么想的。

可是，有些人似乎从来没有过那些想法。他们认为没有什么是做不到的，而且他们乐在其中。他们参加跳伞训练、在非洲丛林探险或者为那些无法解决的问题找寻答案。

他们并不需要富有，也不需要美丽、最聪明或最有天赋。秘密不在于他们拥有什么、在做什么或者他们是谁，而在于他们是怎么想的。

他们

相信。

他们相信他们可以完成任何想做的事,而且没有什么事情是可以不劳而获的。

他们相信担心是多余的,只要一直做下去,事情终究会被解决。

而且他们相信这种锲而不舍的努力过程会提高自身的意志力和耐力,从而使自己有能力应对下一个重大的历险或者挑战。

是什么让这些过着充实美好生活的"能人"们与众不同?

没什么,真的,仅仅是

你相信。

Nothing we do,
however virtuous,
can be accomplished alone;
therefore, we are saved by love.

Reinhold Niebuhr

我们所做的一切，不管有多圣洁，都无法独自完成。因此，我们得救于爱。

勒吼德·呐伯尔

Luke shot a look at his wife. He had no intention of obeying the doctor's orders.

卢克看了他妻子一眼。他不想遵从医生的命令。

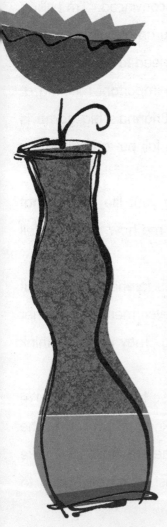

Wouldn't Miss It

A groan escaped Luke's lips as pain shot through his knee. After a restless night of sleep, he'd awakened to realize the injury that he was hoping would simply go away was not only present but getting worse. His wife of forty-eight years, who apparently wasn't sleeping either, asked, "How does it feel? Do you need something?"

"Now, Jo, I'm going to be tine. There's nothing to worry about."

His protective wife didn't seem convinced. "I'm calling Dr. Brown this morning to make you an appointment."

"For heaven's sake, Jo, I don't need to see a doctor." He tried to shrug it off. "I have an important meeting at the office today, and you know Brianna's big game is tonight. I'm not going to let a little fall put a hold on my life."

"Who's talking about stopping your life, and what do you mean 'little fall'? Jack told me how hard you fell on that tile floor yesterday.

Luke slapped his hand over his forehead and slid it down to cover his eyes. "Oh, don't even mention the other realtors. That was so embarrassing. They probably think I'm getting feeble."

"They do not, Luke. But you have to face facts; you're seventy-five years old, and your knee is swollen to the size of a grapefruit." She took on the emphatic tone Luke knew it was useless to fight against. "You are going to

the doctor today."

He gently lowered his swollen leg to the floor and let out an even louder groan. Jo got up as well and headed toward the kitchen.

"I have'n t started me coffee this morning. I guess I overslept," Luke called out. The truth was, he'd woken thirty minutes earlier but was in so much pain he wasn't sure he could even stand, much less go through his morning routine. For the last forty-eight years, he'd had a fresh pot of coffee waiting for Jo every morning, and he knew this small gesture left undone would give away just how bad his knee really was. He needed to downplay his injury just a little longer.

"I've taught all of my children and grandchildren from the time they were little that when you make a promise, you keep it," Luke hollered to Jo from the bathroom. "And I don't plan to start breaking my promises just because of a sore knee." Especially this one. He'd prom ised Brianna he wouldn't miss any of her basketball games this season. This was her senior year,

and her team had made the playoffs. He wasn't about to miss what could be her final game.

"Luke, dear," his wife called back, "we'll discuss it after we see what the doctor says. I just spoke to Dr. Brown's office, and they can get you in later this morning."

"But my meeting with the new realtors is at eleven o'clock."

"I've already called the office, and everyone will be notified that the meeting is being rescheduled. Now let me help you get dressed."

"OK, I'll go," Luke consented, mostly for show. Jo obviously wasn't making this optional. "And I can get dressed by myself, thank you." He insisted at least on that much.

"You've broken your kneecap, Mr. Shackelford," Dr. Brown said solemnly after looking intently at the x-rays. "We're going to try to avoid surgery, but that means absolutely no pressure on that knee for a full six weeks."

"Uh-huh." *I am not going to just sit around and watch the grass grow. I have work to do—ball games to attend!*

"He can walk on crutches though, right?" Jo asked. Luke knew she was trying to reach some compromise.

Dr. Brown shook her head. "Not for a while. I'm going to put his leg in a soft cast, but I want him to stay off of it completely for a full week. Mr. Shackelford, you can get up to go to the bathroom, using the crutches, but that's it. Then we'll see how you're doing, and maybe you can use them to do some very minimal activity until it heals."

With a set in his jaw, Luke shot a glance at his wife. He had no intention of obeying those orders if they meant missing Brianna's game.

Believing the Best

Jo took a long breath, and Luke saw in her face she knew just what he was thinking. As soon as the doctor left the room, she gave him a stern look of her own. "Oh no you're not, don't even think about it. You'll stay home and rest that leg if I have to tie you to your recliner."

The ride home was not a fun one. They spent the entire time arguing about what he was going to do or not do that evening.

"I'll have someone videotape it and bring it to you as soon as the last buzzer sounds," Jo offered. But Luke knew he had leverage here.

"Oh, this from the woman who just two weeks ago dragged herself to a game in spite of a hundred-and-three-degree fever," Luke said with a smirk and a dose of good-natured sarcasm. "I'm not the only one around here who won't take no for an answer."

Sitting in the living room, leg propped up on the ottoman, Luke took up the argument again. "Jo, this is not just about my being stubborn," he said for probably

the fiftieth time that day. "You know how important it is to Brianna that we both be there." But he could see that Jo wasn't budging.

"You heard the doctor's orders. She said NO pressure on your leg. You'd never get into the gym without being jostled or putting weight on it somehow. And where would you sit if you got there? I can't carry you up the bleachers."

"They have handicapped seating you know—" That's it! Why hadn't he thought of that before? "I'll get a wheelchair! " Yes. He'd found a way. "Do we know anyone with an extra wheelchair?"

"Luke, the doctor said for you not to go *anywhere,* and no, we don't know anyone with an extra wheelchair."

"Will you please just bring me the phone book?"

A few minutes later, however, Luke was more discouraged than ever. "I've called all the medical supply rental stores in the phone book, and they're either closed for the day or don't have any more wheelchairs available."

Jo let out a sigh, but this time he detected more sympathy than exasperation. "Dear, Brianna will understand.You're injured. She'll know you'd be there if you could."

"I know, but I wanted her to understand that I'd never break a promise to her." It was six o'clock. The game started at seven, and Luke was feeling like a prisoner in his own home.

"Look, your favorite team is playing on TV," Jo said. Luke knew she was trying to help. But tonight that wasn't going to be enough.

"Jo, even the Oklahoma State Cowboys couldn't distract me this evening." He sighed, finally ready to admit to defeat, when he suddenly had another idea. "Jo! Quick, bring me the phone again."

Her eyes narrowed, and she gave him a wary look as she handed him the phone. "What are you trying now?"

"Just watch and see," he said with a grin.

"Josh, hey, it's Pap. What are you doing right now?"

"Jake and I are getting ready to go watch Brianna's game," his grandson answered. "Hey, sorry about your knee. Are you watching Oklahoma State play tonight?"

"Of course not," Luke retorted. "I'm going to Brianna's game."

"I thought you had doctor's orders to stay off that knee," Josh said.

"I do—that's where you and Jake come in. I need two strong young men to carry me into the game." Luke looked over to his wife. She just shook her head, threw her hands in the air, and walked away. He smiled, knowing she'd forgive him before the

evening was over.

"We'll be there in no time" Josh said.

Luke heard the chants of cheerleaders and the thumps of basketballs as he rode into the gymnasium on the arms of his two grandsons. He didn't care how old or feeble he looked, he was just glad to be there and to have kept his promise.

He settled gingerly into the chair they'd brought from home and managed to catch Brianna's eye as she warmed up. The look of surprise on her face was worth his every effort. She ran over and gave him a big hug.

"What are you doing here?"

"I promised you I'd come—I wouldn't miss it for the world," he said with a smile.

Brianna shook her head and scolded, reminding him of Jo. But she was also transparent like her grandmother, and he could see that she was pleased. "I love you," she said, adding sternly, "but promise me you won't jump up and down when I score all the points." She

flashed him a grin and jogged back onto the court.   Just
before she was out of range, she turned and called over
her shoulder. "I knew you wouldn't miss it! "

不会错过它

膝盖一阵疼痛时，卢克发出一声呻吟。一夜无眠之后，他开始认识到这个伤并不会像他期望的那样容易好转，而是仍在持续着，且情况越来越糟。他58岁的妻子显然也没睡好，问道："感觉怎么样？需要点什么吗？"

"乔，我马上就会康复的，不用担心。"

对他一直呵护备至的妻子似乎并不相信。"我早上打电话给布朗医生预约为你看病。"

"看在上帝的分上，乔，我不需要看医生。"他试着脱身。"我今天办公室有个重要的会议，而且你知道布瑞安娜的关键比赛就在今晚。我可不想让一个小小的跌伤妨碍了我的生活。"

"谁说妨碍你生活了？小小的跌伤是什么意思？杰克已经告诉我昨天你跌到地砖上是多么的重了。"

卢克用手拍了一下他的额头，然后滑下遮住他的眼睛。"哦，别谈另一个房产经纪人了，太尴尬了，他们可能认为我变得虚弱了。"

"他们没那么想，卢克。但你必须要面对现实；你已经75岁了，而且你的膝盖已经肿得像柚子那么大了。"她断然地说道。卢克知道反驳是徒劳的。"你今天要去看医生。"

他轻轻地将肿胀的腿伸到地板上，发出了更大的呻吟声。乔也起床了，朝厨房走去。

"我今天早上还没有煮咖啡呢。我猜我是睡过头了，"卢克大声叫道。实际上他提前半小时就醒了，但疼得太厉害，他不确定自己能否站起来，所以没能坚持一贯的程序。在过去的58年中，他总是在每个早晨喝着一壶新鲜的咖啡，等乔起床。他知道这个小小的未完成的动作反映出他的膝伤是多么的严重。他需要更长的时间来淡化他的伤。

"在我的子女和外孙们还小的时候，我就教过他们要言而有信，"卢克在盥洗室向乔喊道。"我不想仅仅因为一个疼痛的膝盖就开始食言。"尤其是这一次。他已经答应布瑞安娜不会错过她这个赛季所有的篮球比赛。她已经大四了，而且她的队进入了决赛。他不想错过这个可能是她的最后一场比赛。

"卢克，亲爱的，"他妻子回应道，"等医生看过病情之后我们再讨论这件事。我刚刚和布朗医生的办公室通过电话，他们早上迟点就可以过来。"

"但11点我和新房产经纪人有个会议。"

"我已经打电话给办公室了,并通知所有人会议将另期举行。现在让我帮你穿好衣服。"

"好,我去,"卢克同意了,多半是在敷衍。乔显然不会妥协。"我可以自己穿衣服,谢谢。"他至少要坚持那么做。

"你跌碎了膝盖骨,夏克尔福特先生,"布朗医生在仔细地看过X光片后郑重地说道。"我们尽量不去做手术,但这意味着那个膝盖在六周内完全不能负重。

"嗯…"我可不想仅仅是坐在那儿或是盯着小草生长。我有事要做——观看球赛!

"但他可以架着拐杖走路,不是吗?"乔问道。卢克知道她在试着达成一些妥协。

布朗医生摇了摇头。"暂时还不行。我将会给他的腿打上软石膏,但我想让他在一周后拆除它。夏克尔福特先生,你可以起床架着拐杖去盥洗室,但仅限于此。然后我们会看你做得怎么样,或许你可以用它们来做一些最小幅度的活动,直到伤口愈合。"

卢克咬紧了牙根,看了他妻子一眼。如果这些要求意味着错过布瑞安娜的比赛的话,他是不想执行的。

乔长吸了一口气,卢克从她脸上读出她知道他此刻在想什么。医生一离开房间,她就给了他一个严厉的眼神。"噢,不,你别那么做,想都别想。你就待在家,养好腿伤,如果需要的话我会把你绑在

躺椅上。"

回家的路途气氛并不轻松。他们整个时间都在争论他晚上要做什么或者不该做什么。

"我会叫人把比赛录下来，然后结束哨一响我就会把它带给你，"乔说道。但是卢克知道他还可以讨价还价。

"噢，这录像带来自于两周前不顾高热103华氏度而去现场观看比赛的女性，"卢克得意地笑着说道，而且有点善意讽刺的味道。"我不是这儿唯——个不会拒绝的人。"

卢克坐在起居室里，腿撑在褥榻上，再次争论开来。"乔，这并不仅仅是我固执的问题，"这可能是他那天第五十次说那样的话。"你知道我们俩都在现场对布瑞安娜来说有多么重要。"但他也明白乔不会改变主意。

"你听到医生的要求了。她说了腿完全不能负重。不管怎么样，你不可能不受拥挤而进入体育场或者让腿负重。而且如果你去了你坐哪儿呢？我可无法把你扛到露天看台上去。"

"那儿有残疾人专座你知道吗？——"太棒了！为什么之前没有想到呢？"我去拿一个轮椅！"是的，他找到解决办法。"我们知道谁有多余的轮椅吗？"

"卢克，医生说过你哪儿都不能去，而且，我们认识的人中也没有谁有多余的轮椅。"

"请你把电话号码本递给我好吗？"

　　然而,几分钟过后,卢克变得非常沮丧。"我打了号码簿中的所有医学器材租赁店的电话,他们不是今天已经关门了,就是没有多余的轮椅可租。"

　　乔叹了口气,但这次卢克发现她的同情胜过恼怒。"亲爱的,布瑞安娜会理解的。你受伤了。她会知道如果你能去的话你肯定会到场的。"

　　"我知道,但我想让她了解我从来不会对她食言。"已经六点了。比赛七点开始,而卢克感觉到他像一个在自己家中的囚犯一样。

　　"看,电视上正播放你最喜欢的球队呢,"乔说道。卢克知道她正试着帮他,但今晚是不够的。

　　"乔,今晚即使是俄克拉何马州牛仔队也不能转移我的注意力。"他叹气道,在最终准备接受这次失败的时候,他突然有了另一个想法。"乔!快,再把电话拿给我。"

　　她眯起眼睛 递给他电话的同时警惕地看了他一眼。"你现在想试图干什么?

　　"等着瞧吧,"他咧嘴笑道。

　　"乔希,嘿,我是爷爷。你现在在做什么呢? "

　　"我和加克正准备去看布瑞安娜的比赛," 他孙子回答道。"嘿,很遗憾你膝盖受伤了。你今晚看俄克拉何马州的比赛吗? "

　　"当然不,"他快速答道。"我去看布瑞安娜的比赛。"

　　"我原以为你会听医生的话让膝盖好好休息呢,"乔希说道。

　　"是这样的——那就是你和加克可用的地方。我需要两个强

壮的年轻人扛着我去看比赛。"卢克看了他妻子一眼。她只是摇了摇头，挥舞着手臂，然后走开了。他笑了，知道今晚结束之前她会原谅他的。

"我们得立刻到那，"乔希说道。

当他在两个孙子的搀扶下进入体育馆的时候，卢克听到拉拉队队长的叫喊声和篮球的砰砰声。他不管自己年龄多大或者看起来多虚弱，只是很高兴能到现场并遵守诺言。

他小心翼翼地坐进他们从家带来的椅子上，并在布瑞安娜热身的时候努力去引起她的注意。当看到她脸上惊讶的表情的时候，他觉得他的一切努力都是值得的。她跑过来给了他一个紧紧的拥抱。

"你在这做什么？"

"我答应过你我会来——我无论如何都不会错过它，"他笑着说道。

布瑞安娜摇着头责备他，这让他想起了乔。她像她祖母一样直率，而且他看得出她很高兴。"我爱你，"她说道，又严厉地补充道，"但答应我，当我每次得分时，不要跳。"她突然咧嘴一笑，然后慢跑回到场内。就在她即将走出能听到说话声的区域时，她转过身大声地吼道："我早就知道你不会错过它的。"

·chapter seven·

Sharing Memories

7

共享美好的记忆

Today is a day for rejoicing!
Think about what't good,
noble, and right. Reflect on
things that are pure, lovely,
and admirable. Anything
excellent or praiseworthy
warrants memories. Meditate
on all I've done for you, and
consider all My mighty deeds.

Remembering you,
Your God of Joy

—from Psalm 118:24; Philippians 4:8; Psalm 77:12

今天是值得惊喜的日子！想象那些好的、高尚的、正直的事情。回想那些纯真的、可爱的和值得羡慕的事情以及那些美好的值得赞美的回忆。沉思于我为你所做的一切，并思考我有力的行为。

记住你,你快乐的上帝

A one-year-old with her face covered in birthday cake.   An elderly couple holding hands.A snugly, fuzzy kitten. You can't help but smile at these things.

God gives us little gifts just like these every day to smile about—things that make us happy.   Things that brighten our days. Good memories we can use to cheer ourselves and others.   Look back at old photographs.   You probably have some of these cheery memories stored away in a box.   Maybe you're grinning just thinking about them.   Where's that picture of your five-year-old when he discovered the puppy Santa put in his stocking,   or the one of your oldest daughter painting her sister's toenails?

How about the one of you and your husband running through a cascade of rice, eager to start your life

together?

Sometimes our days can get lonely, or tiresome, or too hectic. But if we pay attention, we'll see that God is sprinkling little blessings in our lives. If you feel like you haven't experienced one of these recently, pull out those old photo albums and spend some time remembering.

Life is full of memories—some good, some not so good. Stay focused on the good ones and let the difficult times get a little faded. Then take some of that happiness and the empathy you learned along the way, and share them with others who might need some comfort or just some company. Before you know it, the day will be filled with smiles— yours and theirs.

一张沾满了蛋糕的一岁小脸;一对挽着

手的老夫妇;一只蜷缩着的毛茸茸的小猫咪。这些

总能让你会心微笑。

生活每天都会赐予我们一些这样的小礼物，让我们

微笑,让我们开心,照亮我们的每一天。翻开那些老照

片,美好的回忆总会使你我心情愉悦。也许这些愉悦

的记忆是被收藏在某个盒子里,哪怕仅仅是回想

一下都会忍俊不禁。你是否还记得5岁时圣

诞老人放入你长袜中的那只小狗,抑

或你的大女儿给她妹妹染花的

脚趾甲，又如你拉着爱

人穿出麦浪向往

新生的

场景？

我们的日子有时也会变得寂寞、乏味或者忙乱，但是如果我们用心体会，就会发现生活其实也给予了我们美好和祝福。如果你最近没有感觉到这些美好，那就翻开旧相册，用点时间再重温它们吧。

生活总是充满了回忆，美好的和不那么美好的。记住其中美好的部分，让那些曾经的困扰随时间渐渐褪去。那此后再遇到了需要安慰或是陪伴的人，你就可以撷取快乐与其共同分享，不知不觉，生活便会再次充满微笑——你的和他们的。

God gave us memories
that we we might have
roses in December.

J. M. Barrie

上帝给了我们记忆，使我们能
够记住十二月的玫瑰。

J.M. 拜雷尔

*N*o one had ever knocked on Trudy's door before. It was the sweetest sound she'd heard in a long time.

以前从没人敲过特露蒂的门，这是她听到的最美好的声音。

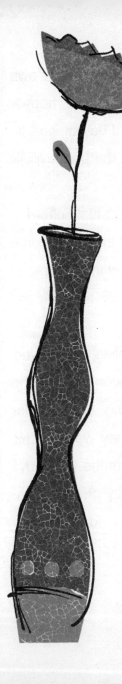

Company

The year was 1962, and Jim and Trudy had only been married four months when Jim proudly announced, "I got a job in North Carolina for the summer. We move in two weeks."

The nineteen-year-old newlyweds had been living in an apartment over Trudy's parents' garage while they were both in college, so they were excited about embarking on this great adventure. Trudy looked forward to having her own place and being the perfect housewife. She happily envisioned Jim coming home from a hard day at work to a clean apartment and a beautiful meal she had lovingly prepared.

Since they didn't own a car and couldn't afford a moving van, they decided to set out for their new home by train. They took only what they could fit in a couple of suitcases, but that didn't bother them. All they needed was each other.

A month after being in North Carolina, however, Trudy was lonely. Jim worked twelve-hour shifts at the plant, so she was alone much of the time. She lived for the weekends, when Jim was off and they would picnic and explore the countryside together. But the weekdays  just seemed to creep by. She did laundry on Mondays, vacuuming and dusting on Tuesdays, and grocery shopping almost every day, trying to spread out her chores.

Trudy missed her family immensely. She missed

everything about home. She missed her friends. She even missed her schoolwork. The only people she really had any contact with were the grocery-store clerks. And she'd found a friend in a gray, long-haired cat that was always hanging around the store. The cat had friendly blue eyes, and Trudy enjoyed when it would rub against her legs as she walked through the door. She always stooped to say hello and to stroke its silky fur.

Trudy walked the three-fourths of a mile to the grocery store even when she didn't need to buy much— or anything at all. She'd spend at least an hour combing the aisles, making small talk with anyone who would join in. "Those cantaloupes look nice and ripe, don't they?" she would ask. She received polite smiles and a few brief replies but never the conversation she longed for.

One day as she stood in the check-out lane, the middleaged man Trudy guessed was the owner of the small market approached her.

"Excuse me, ma'am, I'm George. I've noticed that you come here often and always carry your bag home."

Sharing Memories

Trudy was thrilled just to have someone else initiate an exchange, and this man reminded her of her dad, who called all ladies "ma'am" no matter how old or young they were. "Yes sir, I live less than a mile from here. My husband and I don't have a car, so I make frequent small trips and get just what I can carry."

"I'd be glad to let you borrow a grocery cart if you need it," he offered politely. "My wife could come by your place later and pick it up."

She was excited about the opportunity for some company. At last, maybe she could make a new friend. Trudy didn't really need enough groceries to fill a cart, but she wasn't about to pass up this gracious offer. She thanked him profusely and proceeded to stroll up and down the aisles, buying anything she thought she could use.

She felt a little odd pushing a grocery cart down the sidewalk, but she didn't care. It was a change of pace in her long, monotonous week. She wasn't sure what she would do tomorrow, since she now had enough groceries to last for a while, but she'd figure that out later.

Right now she had big plans to bake a cake, one of those delicious sour-cream pound cakes her mom had taught her to make. She wanted to be prepared for her first visitor.

Later Trudy started when she heard the rap of the doorknocker. No one had ever knocked on her door before, and she was sure it was the sweetest sound she'd heard in a long time. She quickly scanned the tiny apartment to make sure everything was in place, then ran to greet her guest.

"Hi, please come in," she said to the woman with the kindest face she'd ever seen. "I'm Trudy. I'm so glad you came."

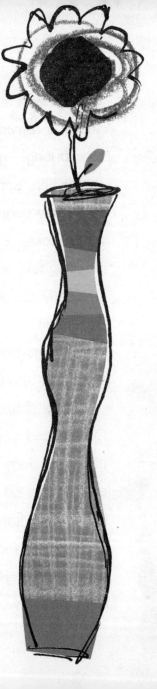

Sharing Memories

"My name is Betty, and it's my pleasure," the store owner's wife said with a smile. She placed the basket she was carrying gently on the floor beside the sofa and took a long, gratifying whiff of the aroma coming from the kitchen. "Something smells wonderful! "

Trudy beamed with pride. "It's my mother's special pound cake. Would you like some? I was hoping you'd sit down and have a piece with me."

Betty sat on the old couch that had come with the apartment as Trudy served her the cake and some tea. "This brings back fond memories of when George and I were first married," she said sweetly.

They chatted awhile, Trudy devouring stories of George and Betty's newlywed life and sharing some of her own. Betty told about meals she had burned, once even setting off the smoke alarm, and about their first move away from home. "It was so hard to leave my family and friends to go where I didn't know anyone but my husband. He spent most of his time trying to earn a living for the two of us, and I felt terribly alone."

Before Trudy could catch herself, tears sprang to her eyes. Somehow it felt soothing to know someone else had felt as she did now.

"George told me he's seen you in the store almost every day. He asked me to pick up the cart and to bring you a little something. It's been more than a few years, but we do remember how it is to be newlyweds and far away from home."

Betty went on to tell Trudy that they had lived in a similar little apartment and that one day, to her surprise and delight, their landlord had broken one of her own rules and had given her a little gray kitten named Sweet Pea to keep her company. "That kitten had the most friendly blue eyes and was the bes little friend to me."

Suddenly making the connection, Trudy gasped. "It can't be. The nice cat from the store?" Did cats live that long?

"Oh, so you've met Dolly. No, she's Sweet Pea's great-great-granddaughter. Sweet Pea's family has grown right along with ours, and that kind landlord

became a lifetime friend of the family too." As Betty talked, she picked up the basket and slowly pulled back a Blanket to reveal a beautiful, tiny, fuzzy, gray kitten curled up and sound asleep.

"Dolly had kittens just six weeks ago. When George told me about you, we agreed right away that you were just the person we wanted to have one of her precious babies—to pass on this blessing of friendship. We wouldn't give her to just anyone."

"Oh! She's beautiful! I'd love to have her. I promise I'll take very good care of her," Trudy gushed, her voice filled with gratitude.

Betty chuckled as she got up to leave. "I know you will. It's always nice to have someone to talk to when you're far away from home. Even if that someone doesn't talk back."She smiled warmly.

"Thank you so much," Trudy said as she kissed her new furry companion on the back of her neck. "And please, Betty, come back again—and here, take a piece of pound cake for your husband. This was so kind of you both."

That night when Jim arrived home, Trudy was curled contentedly on the sofa with the little gray kitten purring happily on her lap. They named her Ally, and she became like a member of the family. George and Betty became like Jim and Trudy's parents away from home, inviting them over often for Sunday lunch during their few months there.

Several years had passed when Trudy walked up the stairs carrying a covered basket. She could hardly contain her smile as she knocked on the apartment door. The stairs weren't as easy to climb as they used to be, and the memories were almost overwhelming when

she was greeted by a smiling young woman she'd met at church the previous Sunday.

"Please,   come in! it's so nice to have some company," she said. "I never realized how lonely it would be moving to a new town all alone."

Trudy entered and gently placed the basket on the floor, hoping the little gray kitten would sleep until she was ready to pull back the blanket.

相伴——分享爱，温暖你·········

　　那是在1962年，吉姆和特露蒂刚刚结婚了4个月。这天，吉姆骄傲地宣布："我在北卡罗莱纳州得到一份暑期工作。我们两周后搬过去。"

　　这对19岁的新人一直住在特露蒂父母车库后的一间小房子里。他们大学还没毕业，所以这次远行让他们异常兴奋。特露蒂一直向往拥有一个自己的小天地，做一个贤妻良母。她开心地想象着，当吉姆劳累了一天回家时，迎接他的是干净整洁的住所和她精心烹制的饭肴。

　　他们没有自己的车，也租不起，最终决定乘坐火车前往新家。他们只带了两个行李箱所能容下的东西，但这并没有使他们担忧，他们在乎的仅仅是有对方相伴。

　　然而，在北卡罗莱纳州住了一个月之后，特露蒂就感到非常孤独。吉姆每天要在工厂里工作12个小时,在这期间,她只能一个人在家里孤单地等候。她期待着每个周末,吉姆休假了,他们便可以一起外出野餐,或者去郊区旅行。但是周末总是来得太慢太慢。周一的时候,她洗衣服;周二打扫卫生;她几乎每天都会去杂货店买东西,希望借此多找点事做。

特露蒂非常想念她的家人,想念家里的一切。她怀念自己的朋友,甚至怀念课程学业。在这里她唯一能打交道的只有杂货店的营业员,而可以称得上朋友的,也只是一只经常在杂货店附近游逛的长毛灰猫。这只猫有着一对友善的蓝眼睛。她喜欢进门的时候,它凑上来蹭她的腿。这时,她都会弯下腰跟它打声招呼,摸一摸它柔滑的毛。

特露蒂家距杂货店有0.75英里远。即便没有什么要买的,她也会去转转。她会花一个多小时在货架前理来理去,与身边所有的人搭讪。她会问:"这些熟的香瓜看起来不错啊,是吧?"身边的人往往报以礼貌的微笑或是简短的回答,但是从没有她期待中的交谈。

一天,她正在排队付账,一个看似商店老板的中年男子走上前来,对她说:"你好,女士,我叫乔治。我注意到你经常光临本店,然后买一袋东西回家。"

特露蒂激动不已,终于有人主动跟她谈话了!这个男人让她想到了自己的父亲,在面对其他女性的时候,不论年龄大小,他都会称呼"女士"。她回答道:"是的,先生。我就住在不到1英里远的地方。我和我的丈夫没有买车,每次来拿不了太多东西,所以需要经

常来。"

"如果你愿意,可以借一辆购物车推走。"他礼貌地提议,"我的妻子可以过会去你住处取回来。"

有机会找到人陪伴,她显得很兴奋。或许,她能结交到一个新朋友。其实特露蒂没有那么多东西要买,但是她并不打算拒绝这个亲切的建议。怀着某种深切的感恩之情,她继续在商店里溜达起来,并买下了所有她认为以后会用得着的东西。

在路上推着一辆购物车行走似乎有些奇怪,但是她不在乎。这个单调冗长的星期终于有了些许变化。她不知道明天还能做点什么,她买的东西足够用好长一阵子的了,但她现在也不去计较了。

眼下她正计划着做一个美味的富油蛋糕,是妈妈曾教给她的一种酸奶蛋糕,想以此迎接她的第一个客人。

没多久,特露蒂就被门环响声惊起。之前从没有人来敲过家门,她感到这是许久以来她所听到的最美妙的声音。她迅速地环视了一遍自己的小屋,确保一切都井然有序,才冲向门口迎接她的客人。

"你好,请进来吧。"她的脸上洋溢着最热情的笑容,"我就是特露蒂,很高兴您能来。"

"我叫贝蒂,也很高兴见到你。"店主的妻子微笑着答道。她把带来的篮子轻轻放在沙发旁,深深吸了一口从厨房飘来的香味,欣喜地说:"真的好香啊!"

特露蒂自豪地笑了起来:"这是我妈妈自制的一种富油蛋糕,

要来点吗？我们坐下尝一尝吧。"

　　然后特露蒂去取了些茶和蛋糕，贝蒂便在房东留下的那个旧沙发上坐了下来。她舒心地说："这又让我想起了刚和乔治结婚的时候。"

　　她们聊了好一会，特露蒂完全沉浸在乔治和贝蒂的新婚故事中，同时也诉说了一些自己的事情。贝蒂讲了她过去烧饭的经历，有一次居然都引发了火警；又提到了他们第一次远离家的感觉："离开家，和我丈夫到了一个举目无亲的地方，那段日子真是太痛苦了。他大部分时间都需要去工作来养活我们俩，而我一个人感到特别的孤独。"

　　不知不觉之中，特露蒂的眼泪已流了下来。知道另一个人也曾有过同样的感受，这让她心里稍稍宽慰了一些。

　　"乔治告诉我，几乎每天都会在杂货店看到你。他让我来取购物车，也希望能给你带来些改变。虽然已经过去很多年了，但是我们一直都记得刚结婚时我们远离家的那段日子是多么的难熬。"

　　贝蒂向特露蒂继续聊起他们曾经住过的一个简朴的小公寓。有一天，终于打破了无聊，发生了一件令她惊讶和欢欣的事情——他们的房东送了一只取名为"甜豆"的小灰猫给她做伴。"它长着一对友善的蓝眼睛，成了我最亲密的朋友。"

　　突然，特露蒂像是联想到了什么，她问道："啊，难道是商店里的那只猫吗？"猫会活这么久吗？

　　"噢，你已见过多利了。它是甜豆的曾曾孙女。甜豆的孩子们

一直跟我们生活在一起，那位善良的房东对它们也非常好。"正说着，贝蒂取过篮子，轻轻掀开上面的小毛毯。里面蜷缩着一只漂亮的、毛茸茸的、灰色的小猫咪，正在呼呼大睡。

"多利6个星期前刚刚生了一窝小猫。当乔治告诉我关于你的情况后，我们马上就意识到，你正是我们想要遇到的人。送给你一只多利的孩子，同时也希望延续这份友谊的祝福。我们并不是什么人都给的哦。"

"噢，它太漂亮了！我非常喜欢它。我保证会照顾好它的。"特露蒂感激得热泪盈眶。

贝蒂站起来告别，微笑着说："我知道你会的。当一个人远离家的时候，总是希望能有个人说说话，即使对方仅仅是在听也好。"

"太感谢你了。"特露蒂吻了吻她的新伙伴的绒毛，"贝蒂，以后一定再来啊。还有，请把这块蛋糕带给你的丈夫。非常感谢你们两位的好意。"

当晚吉姆回家的时候，特露蒂正惬意地缩在沙发里，腿上趴着一只呼噜呼噜欢叫的小灰猫。他们给它取名叫"艾丽"，把它当成家里正式的一员。乔治和贝蒂则像他们的父母一样，在剩下的几个月里，经常邀请他们周日去家里共进午餐。

几年后的一天，特露蒂也带了个盖着的篮子，走上台阶。手刚敲在门上，脸上已露出了笑容。这段台阶已经不像以前那样好走了。当门开的时候，她不禁思绪万千。迎接她的是一个年轻的姑娘，

她们是上周日在教堂里遇到的。

"你好,快请进！真高兴能有人来陪我。"她说,"我从没想到一个人搬到这个陌生的城镇后,会如此的寂寞。"

特露蒂进了门,轻轻地把篮子放在地上,心里想,不知道过会儿掀开毯子的时候,小灰猫是不是还在睡着呢?